FROZEN IN PARADISE

A DESTINATION DEATH MYSTERY

CHARLEY MARSH

TIMBERDOODLE PRESS

Timberdoodle Press

P.O. Box 194

Houston, MN 55943

timberdoodle@goacentek.net

Print Book ISBN# 978-1-945856-71-6

Cover Art: nordenworks.gmail.com /depositphotos.com

CHAPTER ONE

Harriet Monroe, Public Relations Director for the Island Resort, chided herself for losing track of the time. She was scheduled to meet with the resort's world famous chef Simon Fritola . . . ten minutes ago.

"Crap, crap, crap."

She groaned and began to jog slowly along the pink crushed shell road that connected the south end of the island to the north end. It figured that on a day when she needed one of the resort's golf carts that were found *everywhere* for anyone's use there wasn't a single one in sight.

Harriet ran nearly every day on the beach after work but trying to run in a skirt and moderately heeled sandals was far more difficult and just wrong.

She slowed back down to a walk. There was no point in arriving all hot and sweaty and disheveled. Mr. Fritola would not appreciate it. She had called him and apologized for running late and hoped his scowl was for something happening in the kitchen and not directed at her personally.

Despite feeling stressed over her late start Harriet couldn't resist taking the time to appreciate the beauty of the tropical island. She'd arrived three months before and still marveled over how different it was from her native New England.

Sugar fine white sand separated the road from the sun-speckled turquoise water on her left. Lush jungle plants filled with colorful birds, lizards, and insects bordered the road on her right. Large, exotic blossoms perfumed the air and coconut palms soared overhead.

The gentle whoosh of waves lapping the shore accompanied a symphony of birdsong. It made her smile to realize that she could pick out a few individual tunes.

She approached her office but didn't stop, skirting around the pale stone building to the kitchen building behind it. All of the buildings on the resort were built from the same pale limestone and ranged in color from white to soft yellow.

Every building on the island was also built to withstand a Category Five tropical storm. Easily replaced thatching disguised solid concrete roofs that made the buildings strong as bunkers.

No expense had been spared in constructing the resort by its owner Douglas Wade, the wealthiest man on the planet. Wade was also a recluse. Harriet hoped to meet him one day to thank him for hiring her and for all he'd done for her since.

She pulled open a wide, carved wooden door and entered the kitchen building's small courtyard. Open to the sky, the unusual entry held a round, dark stone fountain with three bronze dolphins arcing out of the top. Water spouted from the creatures' mouths, cascading down several tiered catch-basins. Small peach and green plumed lovebirds flitted in the fountain's middle tier, picking up tiny insects with soft chitters.

Large, perfumed, tropical flowers in brilliant reds, pinks,

and yellows grew around the courtyard's edges and three palm trees stretched far above the roof edge. There were several seating areas with cane chairs and small round glass tables for the kitchen staff's breaks. To Harriet's eyes the peaceful courtyard looked like a small zen garden.

While the Island Resort provided over the top luxury for its guests, it hadn't neglected the staff who looked after those guests and made sure the place ran smoothly. The staff housing was well above average and working conditions were enviable. She felt incredibly blessed to be working there.

Remembering how late she was, Harriet hurried across the courtyard and through a door opposite the entrance. A short, functional, white-tiled corridor led her to the resort's largest kitchen–the strictly-run domain of Chef Fritola.

She found the world renowned chef standing in the center of the spotless white tiled room with his arms crossed over his chest, scowling at everyone. Tall and portly, the famous chef wore his silver streaked black hair slicked back into a ponytail. His dark brown eyes darted everywhere and missed nothing.

Chef was master and commander of his domain and his loud baritone voice made sure everyone within shouting distance knew it. Harriet had been thoroughly intimidated by the chef the two times they'd met in person.

She sucked in a deep breath and squared her shoulders now as she prepared to confront him for the third time.

"Third time's a charm," she whispered. The man had no power over her, she reminded herself. She had no reason to fear him. They were equals in the resort's employee hierarchy.

Dozens of droids and humans, all dressed in resort-blue double breasted chef coats and toques, worked at the three long rows of stainless tables that dominated the center of the kitchen. Some chopped vegetables on large wooden cutting boards, some fed freshly made doughs through pasta machines.

In an alcove off to one side a man wrapped in a bloody apron butchered a large meaty leg Harriet couldn't identify on a thick wooden slab. The sight made her feel slightly nauseated and she focused on the droids washing leafy greens at the food only sinks instead.

The room smelled of yeast and fresh herbs and roasting meat and blood.

A row of industrial dishwashers and several more sinks big and deep enough to hold a large adult man sat against the wall to Harriet's left. One long wall held a row of eight burner gas stoves, six double stacked built-in ovens, and several charcoal grill tops.

An old-fashioned wood-fired oven took up one corner. Wood fired ovens were rare, found only in exclusive restaurants that could charge enough to cover the cost of the wood fuel since cutting trees for firewood was prohibited worldwide. The wood fired pizza made here had quickly become one of Harriet's favorite meals.

Several chefs dressed in head chef whites stood before the stoves or barked out orders to the blue-coated staff working at the prep tables.

Two pair of huge stainless doors on the fourth wall lead to the industrial chillers.

To Harriet the scene looked chaotic, but she knew that the flashing knives, leaping flames, and abundance of activity was actually a finely choreographed dance orchestrated by Chef Fritola. Chef would accept nothing less.

She stepped into the fray and approached the regal ruler of all she saw.

"Chef. I apologize again for keeping you waiting."

Chef Fritola turned his scowl her way. "I don't have time

to waste, Ms. Monroe. As you can see I am a very busy man. My constant attention is needed to ensure that every morsel that leaves my kitchen is perfect."

Harriet looked around the kitchen. The staff was hopping, it was true. But Chef was doing little more than standing around and terrifying his crew as far as she could tell.

"Of course, Chef." There was no point in arguing. She needed to maintain a civil relationship with the man since she had several publicity ideas for the resort that involved the restaurants.

"This shouldn't take up much of your time," she continued. "I simply want to verify that the ice sculptures for the Pelookie anniversary dinner are correct." She saw Fritola stiffen and knew she'd said the wrong thing. Damn temperamental chefs anyway!

"I'm sure they're superb, Chef," she added quickly. "I expect nothing less from you, but I wouldn't be doing my job if I didn't check on them myself. You understand, surely. I'm sure you are the same way with everything that leaves your kitchen."

The chef looked mollified and Harriet breathed a sigh of relief. Coddling temperamental co-workers was not one of her strong suits.

She followed Chef to the left set of stainless chiller doors. He punched in a code which she knew meant that the freezer hadn't been opened yet that morning. The set of doors to the huge walk-in refrigerator were in constant use, but no one had needed anything from the freezer.

That was a good thing as far as Harriet was concerned. The four large ice sculptures for the Pelookie party were fragile and had taken nearly a week for Chef to make. If one was damaged there was no time left to replace it. The Pelookie anniversary party was scheduled for that evening.

One hundred family members and close friends had descended on the resort for a week-long celebration culminating with tonight's party. Many of the resort's staff would be happy to see them go. The Pelookies had a tendency to be demanding and autocratic.

An icy blast of air hit Harriet as the chef opened the door, making her shiver. She should have thought to grab a sweater or a jacket, she thought ruefully. Her silk suit that was perfect for the island's mild temperatures offered little protection against the sub-zero temps of the industrial freezer.

A row of LED lights set in the center of the freezer's ceiling snapped on when the door opened, lighting a ghostly fog that formed as soon as the cold air met the warm, moist air of the kitchen.

Stainless steel shelving lined the walls to the left and right. The shelves were filled with plastic containers and boxes, contents unknown to Harriet. The air had a slightly stale, chemical odor to it.

Chef Fritola moved deeper into the freezer with Harriet right behind him. She crossed her arms over her chest, hoping to retain some of her body heat. Damn, it was cold.

"You'll see that I did a superb job on the ice sculptures, Ms. Monroe."

"Call me Harry, please, Chef. Everyone else does." Not realizing that he'd stopped, she bumped into Chef's back.

"Sorry, Chef. I wasn't watching where I was going."

A strangled sound came from the man in front of her.

"Chef? Are you all right?"

Chef turned around and grabbed Harriet's arms. His mouth gaped open and his eyes were wide. "It's-it's–"

"Chef?" Harriet pulled her arms free and stepped around the chef's large body to see what had upset him. Had someone broken one of the ice sculptures?

"Oh no. No, no, no." Harriet shook her head as she reached into her knapsack with trembling hands for her link. It didn't work inside the freezer so she hurried back into the kitchen and jabbed number two on her autodial.

"Alex? I think you'd better come over to the kitchens right away."

Harriet turned to look inside the freezer again.

"Come as soon as you can. There's a body in the freezer."

CHAPTER TWO

Harriet felt an urge to get away from the noisy kitchen and decided to wait for Alex back in the kitchen's courtyard. She told Chef Fritola to close and lock the freezer until the security director arrived.

Taking a seat at one of the small tables beside the fountain, Harriet dropped her head into her hands. Another death. After two traumatic deaths during her first month on the job, the last two months had been blissfully peaceful, without incident other than the usual problems one ran into getting a complex resort up and running.

She groaned and flopped back in the chair. A brilliant emerald green gecko eyed her from his upside down perch on a nearby palm.

"Be thankful that your biggest problem is finding something to eat and not becoming a meal for something else," she told it.

There had been jokes among the staff that the Island Resort should be renamed "Destination Death" after the second death occurred. That talk had completely died down, but Harry knew that this new death would revive it.

Who was the poor man? She'd only had a quick glimpse of him. The two images that stuck in her mind were bare feet with blue toes and frost on the man's eyelashes.

"Harriet?" A large warm hand landed on her shoulder.

Harriet leaped to her feet and wrapped her arms around the six-three security director's waist, burying her face in his neck.

His slightly crooked nose and a scar through his right eyebrow made Alex look like a sexy thug, but Harriet knew better. Alex Hayes was the gentlest, most trustworthy person she knew. He was also a crackerjack detective.

She squeezed him tight, grateful for his warmth. "Alex! I didn't hear you come in. I'm so glad you're here. Some poor man got trapped in the industrial freezer and froze to death."

Alex took a long minute to hold her. They had been to bed together one time nearly two months before, an incredible experience he hoped to repeat. But in a move that surprised even him, Alex had put the brakes on, insisting that they date and get to know each other better before they slept together again.

It hadn't taken long for Alex to fall in love with the tall blonde, but he wanted Harriet to be sure of her feelings toward him. Not only had she been badly burned by her ex fiancé before she came to work for the resort, but she had no memories before the age of eight.

He loosened his arms and lifted Harriet's chin, checking her large silver blue eyes for any signs of distress. "Another body, huh? Why are you always the one to find them?"

Harriet shook her head ruefully and gave a small smile. "I seem to be jinxed that way. I'd never even seen a dead body before coming to this island. Now I can't seem to get away from them."

"You don't have to go back to the kitchen with me. I can interview you later."

"No. I'd better come with you. Chef Fritola looked pretty shaken up when I left him. I just needed to get away from the hustle-bustle for a minute."

She stepped away from Alex and slung her worn canvas knapsack over her shoulder. "Hopefully this one will be a straight forward accident."

Alex held the door to the corridor open for her. "I wouldn't bet on it," he said as she passed by him.

It amazed her that even with a newly discovered body in the freezer nothing looked any different in the kitchen. Humans and droids still chopped, washed vegetables, cooked, and cleaned pots and pans.

Ah, one thing had changed. The butcher had finished cutting up the leg he had been working on and now had out a grinder and was feeding chunks of meat into it.

Chef Fritola still stood in the center of the kitchen with his arms crossed over his chest but he looked nowhere near as fierce as he had when she first arrived. His face had paled under his swarthy skin.

"Chef," Alex said as he held out a hand to shake. "I hear you have a small problem with the large walk-in freezer."

Chef grimaced. "You might say that. Excuse me for a moment."

He walked over to a skinny, mocha-skinned male who had just smashed a coconut with a small hammer. Pieces of shell and meat and coconut water had flown everywhere.

The kitchen suddenly grew much quieter. Harriet noticed that the humans were giving Chef sideways looks. The droids worked on, unaffected by the incident.

Chef took the hammer from the man's trembling hand. "How anyone can get a job in a tropical island kitchen and not know the correct way to open a coconut is beyond me," he muttered loud enough for Harriet to hear.

She felt sure that he intended everyone to hear and felt a

wave of dislike for the chef for embarrassing the hapless worker.

"Listen up, people," Chef said loudly. "I am going to demonstrate the correct way to open a coconut, once and once only. The next person who makes a mess of it is fired." He turned to the young man. "Pay close attention."

Chef Fritola held the coconut over a large stainless bowl and tapped the middle of the coconut shell gently but firmly, rotating the shell in his hand until a crack appeared. He gave one more tap and separated the two halves, catching the coconut water in the bowl. The whole process took less than fifteen seconds.

"Think you can handle that?"

"Yes, Chef."

"Good. Don't mess up again." Chef walked over to where Alex and Harriet waited. "I'll open the freezer door for you but I really don't want to go back in there."

"That won't be necessary, Chef. Don't leave the kitchen, though. I'm sure I'll have questions for you."

Alex grabbed the freezer door handle once it was unlocked. "One thing, Chef. Did you recognize the body?"

Chef Fritola nodded. "Yes. It is my sister's boy." He turned and walked over to the giant stoves and began looking in bubbling pots.

"Crap." Alex ran a hand through his hair. "You can wait out here, Harriet. I won't be long. You aren't dressed for the temperatures in there."

"Neither are you," Harriet pointed out. "Besides, I came here to check on the ice sculptures for the Pelookie party tonight and I still need to do that. Especially if the freezer is about to become a crime scene."

"Fine. Just don't touch anything."

Harriet rolled her eyes at Alex's broad back as she followed him inside the freezer. Goose bumps immediately rose on her bare arms. Clouds of fog formed in front of their faces and disappeared. The freezer felt even colder than a Maine winter's night.

"Where are the ice sculptures?" Alex asked.

"Uh, I'm not sure. I saw the body and immediately turned around and left." She skirted around the body, careful not to look down at it. "Here they are."

The four large ice sculptures sat towards the back wall of the freezer on individual rolling tables. The busts represented the four founding members of the Pelookie family business. Three male heads and one female all looked up at her with sightless eyes.

The three male faces showed the same square jaw and broad forehead along with the narrow, beaked nose that Harriet had come to associate with the Pelookie blood kin.

The lone female looked beautiful and regal.

Alex stepped beside her. "Chef Fritola did these?"

"Yes. Now that I know Chef has this hidden talent I'll be calling on him for other special occasions."

Alex frowned at the sculptures. "Siblings?"

"Yes and no. Three brothers and the wife of the eldest brother."

The likeness to the photos that the daughter had sent to Harriet was impressive except for one thing. The woman sported a large, red, capital A painted on her forehead.

"Chef did a great job but I'll have to ask him about the A on the woman," Harriet said, puzzled. "We never talked about it but one of the Pelookie's might have requested it."

Harriet took a deep breath, let it out in a cloud of fog that made her look like a fire breathing dragon, and made herself turn and look closely at the body. He was younger than she had initially thought.

"Poor man." She frowned. "Why are his feet bare?"

"When people suffer from hypothermia their bodies tell

them strange things. There's less oxygen getting to the brain so they hallucinate and can't think straight. At a certain point nerve damage makes some feel as if they're over-heating instead of freezing and they often rip off their clothes."

"I don't see any shoes," Harriet pointed out.

"Yeah, that's a problem. Why would a kitchen worker enter the freezer in bare feet? I'd better call Fox. I'm going to need some help."

They waited outside the freezer until Alex's assistant, an ex-Boston cop named Tarbell Fox, arrived. He handed Alex and Harriet heavy sweatshirts. "I thought these might come in handy."

Harriet smiled to herself over the fact that Tarbell had assumed she'd be helping them find out why a man had frozen to death in the industrial freezer. The way he had naturally included her gave her a warm and fuzzy feeling toward the ex cop.

Then she considered the reason *why* Fox had assumed she'd be involved and the warm and fuzzy feeling went away. She had been too closely involved with the last two resort deaths. She definitely didn't want to be involved with this one.

"Ever deal with a hypothermia victim before?" Alex asked Fox as he pulled the sweatshirt over his head.

"Once. Found a bottle baby frozen in a snowbank. Looked like she'd decided to take a seat and just never got up again. Coroner had to put her into the wagon with her legs and arms bent."

"You found a baby frozen in a snowbank?" Harriet asked, horrified. "Who would do such a thing to their child?"

Fox smiled at her. "A bottle baby is a drunk, Harry. This one was an old lady, a known alcoholic who usually closed down the neighborhood bar on a nightly basis. My theory is that she had a little too much fun and stopped to rest on the way home and most likely passed out."

He shrugged one shoulder. "It happens more often than you'd think. Not just to drunks. Druggies too. We had a few frozen stiffs every winter but Agatha Ramp was the only one I dealt with personally."

"What a horrible way to go." Harriet shuddered.

Fox shrugged again. "I don't know about that. I'm told they simply go to sleep and never wake up. Seems like a fairly painless way to die. I'm told that responsible aquarium owners put sick or unwanted fish in their freezers. It's supposed to be a humane way to euthanize them."

Alex had heard enough. "Thanks for that information. Let's get this done." He opened the freezer door and stepped inside.

"Will we be able to get out of here once the door closes?" Fox asked. He looked behind them at the busy kitchen. "It'd be a shame if no one noticed we were stuck in here."

"Good question." Alex stepped back into the kitchen and spoke to Chef. He came back a moment later with a puzzled frown on his face.

"Chef says the door handle works from the inside but occasionally it freezes and doesn't work. If that happens there's an emergency button beside the door that sets off an annoyingly loud horn in the kitchen. He claims the emergency horn is loud enough to be heard outside the building, and can definitely be heard from his apartment above."

Fox checked the inside door handle. It didn't budge. He dropped to one knee to take a closer look. "Look at this Alex. Someone jammed a piece of metal in the handle so it can't lift up and release."

"Why didn't the victim use the emergency button if he was trapped in here?" Harriet asked. She pointed to the big red button beside the door. "You can't miss it."

Fox pushed the button. Nothing happened. He pulled a multi-purpose tool from his pocket and pried the cap off the button, revealing the inner wiring. Probing gently with his finger, he pulled a loose wire free.

"Looks like it was disconnected and the cover put back on so no one would notice."

The two men looked at each other. "Well, crap," Alex said. "That means we have a murder, not an accidental death."

CHAPTER THREE

After finding the disabled alarm, Alex put a hand on Harriet's arm. "I want you to wait outside the freezer. The less we mess with a potential crime scene the better. We'll prop the door slightly open but if it closes we'll need you to let us out."

Harriet didn't mind waiting for the two men in the warm kitchen. The freezer was kept between minus ten and zero degrees Fahrenheit–much too cold for her comfort, even with the sweatshirt. She spotted Chef Fritola across the room pulling a tray of scones from an oven and walked over to speak with him.

"Chef, did one of the Pelookies ask you to add the red A to Adelaide Pelookie's ice sculpture? Are the others supposed to have their initials added as well?"

"What?" Chef whirled around, almost clipping Harriet with the hot pan. "What are you talking about?"

Red bits of cranberry and deep purple blueberries poked through the tops of the scones. They smelled delicious. Harriet had missed breakfast and itched to try one, but she knew better than to take one without Chef offering first.

"There's a large, red letter A painted on Adelaide's forehead. I wondered who asked you to put it there. It's not in my original instructions for the busts."

The pan of scones slammed onto the nearest counter and Chef Fritola stalked across the kitchen to the freezer but when he reached the door he hesitated. He turned instead and glared at everyone in the kitchen.

"Who messed with my ice sculptures?" he shouted. "When I find who did this I will fire you and make sure you never work in a kitchen again."

Everyone stopped what they were doing when Chef spoke but immediately went back to work. A few shrugged. Most looked perplexed, Harriet noticed. She doubted any of the kitchen staff knew what the chef was talking about. Was the scarlet A why Arlo had entered the freezer?

Chef stalked back over to Harriet and began lifting scones from the pan to a cooling rack. Large flakes of sugar glittered on their tops like tiny shards of ice.

An image of Arlo's open eyes rimmed with frost popped into Harriet's brain.

"I'm sorry about your nephew, Chef. Were you close?"

One large shoulder lifted and fell but Chef didn't look at her. "Some. Not really." He sighed and stared down at the scones. His blunt-nailed fingers drummed the stainless counter top.

"I hadn't seen Arlo in at least ten years before he came here. He's my youngest sister's kid. *Was* my youngest sister's kid. Arlo meant well but he didn't know what he wanted to be when he grew up and he drifted from job to job. He'd get excited about something and go all in and then lose interest. This was the latest stop on his career path."

"He couldn't have been here long, you yourself only started what–about two months ago?"

Chef gave a sharp nod. "Arlo started last week. He was still in that eager to please frame of mind and he was doing well. I was hopeful that he'd finally found the thing he was meant to do. I would have taught him everything I know." His voice thickened.

Harriet reached out and gave the chef's beefy arm a gentle squeeze. "I'm so sorry for your loss, Chef. Arlo was very fortunate to have you."

Chef muttered a thanks and walked away, but not before Harriet saw the sheen in his eyes that told her he was fighting back tears. A minute later he was scolding a sous chef for cutting matchstick carrots too large.

Harriet wandered back over to the freezer just as Alex and Fox came out. They slapped at their arms and stamped their feet to get their circulation revving again. Alex's thick dark lashes held tiny crystals of frost. His deep blue eyes were sad.

"How long do you think someone could survive in there?" Fox asked him.

"The way he was dressed?" Alex thought for a moment. "Less than an hour, I would think, but I'm not an expert. I'm going to call Dr. Clarke at the spa and ask her to take a look at the body. If she can do the autopsy we'll get results a lot faster than waiting for a mainland doctor to get to it."

"Did you learn anything about what happened to Arlo?" Harriet looked from one to the other.

"Arlo? Was that his name? He didn't have any i.d. on him." Alex closed the freezer door. "Until we do an autopsy and get a tox screen we won't know if someone killed him first and dumped the body in there or if he walked in voluntarily."

"Or walked in under duress," Fox pointed out. "Arlo's shoes didn't walk out by themselves."

Harriet told them the little she'd gleaned from talking with chef. "He's hiding it well, but I think Chef Fritola honestly cared for his nephew," she added.

Alex left them to see if the kitchen needed anything from

the freezer before he put it off limits, leaving Fox and Harriet to walk outside together.

Harriet liked the burly Irishman. Intelligence shone in his bright green eyes. He kept his square face clean shaven, his red hair trimmed ultra short, and his clothing neatly pressed. Other than his penchant for confusing her with early twentieth century jazz terms, she found his thought processes to be very linear, something she appreciated.

Alex had told her that Fox had been a good cop who got a raw deal when he was forced to kill a junkie in self defense. The junkie turned out to be related to the Boston mayor's wife and Fox was forced out of his job with no hope of being rehired onto another police force.

Harriet knew that even though the two men had only been working together for a few months, Alex not only respected Fox, he also valued his opinions.

"What do you think, Tarbell? Crazy accident or murder?" she asked as they stood outside the kitchen building in the bright sun. The day had progressed to late morning and the temperatures were a pleasant mid-eighties. Harriet's silk skirt suit ruffled in the gentle breeze. Fox still wore a sweatshirt.

He shook his head at her question. "Definitely murder, but I don't think it was some blowtop. There is something that is too calculated about it."

"Blowtop? I've heard you use that term before but I don't know what it means."

Fox grinned at her. "A blowtop is a crazy or violent person. Someone you expect to blow at any moment. You know–blow their top. Best to avoid them."

"I should have been able to figure that one out for myself." A resort cart turned the corner around Harriet's office building and headed toward them.

"That looks like Dr. Clarke now." Harriet watched the

stylish blue and chrome vehicle approach with the spa's on-site physician at the wheel, still dressed in her white spa lab coat.

Dr. Clarke pulled up and hopped out of the cart, gave a curt nod to Harriet, and asked Fox to take her to the body.

Harriet wasn't offended by the doctor's brusque manner. She knew the woman was busy at the spa and she probably wasn't at all happy to have another dead body to deal with. The doctor had given up a busy practice on the mainland when she felt herself burning out and took the spa job as an antidote. It was unlikely that she had anticipated dealing with dead bodies as part of the job.

Harriet realized there was nothing more that she could do at the kitchen. She might as well head into her office.

CHAPTER FOUR

Harriet followed the same path Dr. Clarke's resort cart had taken around to the front of her building and entered.

"Good morning, Harry." Handsome Jeeves, smartly turned out in an impeccable white linen suit and blue shirt with a matching hankie peeking from a breast pocket, greeted Harriet in a slight English accent and with a bright smile.

It had taken her weeks to train the droid to use her nickname, but he still insisted on calling her Miss Harriet if anyone else was around.

She smiled back at Jeeves and took a few minutes to chat. While most people considered droids to be mere machines, one step up from their autochefs or cars, Harry found that the higher class of droids used on the island had personalities and were as individual as people. She liked them and always gave them the respect she felt they deserved.

Jeeves unlocked the hall door that led to the offices and locked it again behind her.

The wide, cream-tiled hallway was lined with tinted tall narrow windows on her left and colorful frescoes painted by a local artist on her right. The door to her office was neatly camouflaged at the base of a forested mountain, the security panel hidden in the froth of a slim waterfall.

It wasn't until she was alone in her office that the full import of the morning hit her. She kicked off her sandals and walked across the light bamboo floor of the large airy space, stopping beside a wall covered floor to ceiling with book-shelves that were still mostly empty.

She picked up the cherry framed holo of her parents, all that she had left of them. Her beautiful mother stood smiling, wrapped in the arms of a tall, handsome man with silver blue eyes and a strong chin. The same eyes and chin Harriet saw whenever she looked in a mirror.

The couple looked happy and in love. They laughed out at her, forever frozen together in that moment. Not for the first time, she wondered who had taken the holo.

"Morning, Mom. Morning, Daddy. I miss you guys."

A low dull ache started to throb at the back of Harriet's skull. She set the holo down with a sigh and headed for her desk to dig out a pain blocker. She'd had migraines for as long as she could remember, altho unlike some migraine sufferers she'd read about, hers came on suddenly and left just as suddenly.

By the time she'd found the blockers the pain had disappeared so she left them in the drawer. She fired up her desk PC but had trouble focusing on her current project. Images of Arlo's frozen body kept intruding.

Restless, she stood and unlocked and opened the office's lanai doors. Leaning on the door frame, she lifted her face to the sun. A soft onshore breeze carried the pleasant scent of salt and sand and fragrant flowers.

A group of a dozen kids Harriet recognized as part of the Pelookie family carried boogie boards and wave skimmers down to the water, laughing and talking loudly.

She wondered what it would be like to feel that carefree. She had been living on the streets of Portland at their age, struggling to survive.

The broad expanse of white sand between her office and the water was never crowded and even with the group of kids, that morning was no exception. The resort strictly limited the number of guests allowed on the island at any one time in order to ensure that no part of the island–or any of its world class facilities–were crowded.

Even though it had only been open a few months, the Island Resort already had a reputation as the finest resort destination on or off planet. If it wasn't for the dead bodies that kept turning up her job as public relations director would be a snap.

Harriet turned away from the lanai but left the doors open. Thinking about poor frozen Arlo had reminded her that she had an ice sculpture with a bright letter A on the forehead and no time to create a replacement.

It had taken Chef Fritola a solid day and a half to carve just one of the ice busts. He couldn't possibly do one in a few hours while managing the kitchens.

Besides the main kitchen that supplied the restaurants and kept the guest cabins supplied, the head chef oversaw a second, smaller kitchen that fed the resort's employees and handled room service orders. He had a massive responsibility. The old saying that an army marches on its stomach applied to the resort as well.

Word about Arlo would spread like wildfire through the resort. She had learned on her first day there that it was impossible to keep a secret on the island. Harriet decided to tag the resort manager and give her a heads up but she was already too late with the news.

Cass glared at Harriet when she answered her office link.

"What were you thinking, Harry? You found another damn body?"

She pointed a long fingernail painted with purple and yellow zebra stripes at Harriet. The resort manager loved color, the brighter the better.

"This finding of dead bodies fetish of yours has to stop. It took a month for the media bullshit from the last body to die down and now it's going to start up all over again. You're giving the resort a bad rep."

Harriet glared back at her friend. "It's not my fault and you know it. I don't go looking for dead people, Cass. They just turn up."

Cass harrumphed. "I know you don't go looking for trouble, but crikey Harry, you always manage to find it. What is it about you?"

Still feeling a little prickly, Harriet crossed her arms over her chest. "I called to give you a heads up but since you've already heard about it I need to get back to work."

"Yeah, yeah. Keep me posted on what that hunky boyfriend of yours is doing about this latest fiasco, okay?"

A warm glow spread through Harriet's chest at hearing Alex tagged as her boyfriend and a grin creased her face. "I'll tell you what I can. Bye."

She cut the link and sat back in her chair thinking about Alex until the link buzzed again a few minutes later. Jeeves' face filled the screen.

"Payson Douglas is here to see you, Miss Harriet."

It was Thursday, which meant her standing lunch date with Payson, a year round resort resident and close friend of the resort's owner, Douglas Wade.

She'd have to tell Payson about finding Arlo so he could let Mr. Wade know. *If* Wade didn't know already, that was. While none of the staff had met him in person, Mr. Wade

seemed remarkably well informed about everything that
went on at the resort.

"Thank you, Jeeves. Tell Payson I'll be right out." She took
a minute to close and lock the lanai doors and slipped her
sandals back on. Going barefoot while in her office was a bad
habit but one she seemed unable to break–even though she'd
left the building several times without her shoes and had had
to hurry back for them.

Fox had caught her leaving once and pointed to her bare
feet. What had he called her? Boogie-something. Boogity-
boogity. That was it. When she asked him what it meant he'd
smiled and told her the phrase meant hasty and
disorganized.

She grimaced at the thought. Definitely not the image she
wanted to project to her employer's close friend. Fortunately
Payson seemed to honestly like her and had been nothing but
supportive since her arrival–despite the fact that she kept
turning up dead bodies.

CHAPTER FIVE

Harriet hurried out to the lobby to greet Payson. The older man had become very dear to her in the short time she'd lived on the island and she hated to keep him waiting even though she knew that he would never chide her for it.

"Good morning, Harry. It's a pleasure to see you, my dear. You look as lovely as ever." Payson's pale blue eyes twinkled as he greeted her in the lobby.

Harriet's shoulders slumped. "You know already, don't you?"

"About you finding a body in the freezer? Yes, Alex called me right after you notified him. You certainly have a knack for locating the dead, haven't you?"

Harriet scowled. "Cassidy just said the same thing to me. I swear I don't go looking for dead people. They're just . . . " She waved a hand. ". . . they're just there."

It was past time to change the subject. "Where are we lunching today?"

Payson took Harriet's elbow and guided her to the door. "Under the circumstances I thought we'd do something a little special today. I've reserved us a table at the rooftop restaurant."

"The circumstances being me finding another dead body," Harriet said dryly.

"Well it is your third one in as many months. You must admit that it is a little unusual. Only cops and autopsy doctors see that many bodies in a short space of time."

Worried, Harriet glanced sideways at her companion. "Do you think Mr. Wade will feel compelled to fire me?"

Payson stopped and gently turned her to face him. He placed both hands on her shoulders and looked into her eyes.

"Listen to me, Harriet Monroe. Douglas is more than pleased with the job you've been doing as public elations director for the resort. He understands that conditions have been difficult. In spite of that you've found a way to give the resort a positive spin and firmly placed us at the top of vacation destinations. There are no complaints. Trust me, I'd know if there were."

Harriet let out a big sigh. "Thank you, Payson. That makes me feel better. Truly."

"Good." He offered his arm. "Now let's go enjoy our meal. I look forward to my weekly lunch date with the resort's most attractive PR expert."

Laughing and shaking her head at the absurd flattery, Harriet took the offered arm and let Payson lead her to the hotel.

A short while later they were seated at a corner table in the open air restaurant that occupied the entire roof of the south wing of the hotel. A four foot high clear acrylic wall topped with a brass rail offered protection from falls and an unobstructed view of the ocean to the west and the three jungled mountains that dominated the skyline to the east.

A thatched pergola covered half the space, supported by bamboo struts nearly a foot in diameter. Because the building only stood two stories high, trees and vines covered with deep red and orange blossoms towered over the diners, creating the impression that they were dining in a tree house.

Harriet was happy to see that the restaurant was three-quarters full, the diners happy and relaxed, enjoying their food and the spectacular views.

Large, colorful parrots flew and called among the tree-tops in accompaniment to the soft jazz playing through hidden speakers. The scent of the sea blended with the smell of grilled seafood and exotic flowers.

They placed their orders with the waitress and sipped on tart and sweet fresh lemonade while they waited for their food. Slowly the atmosphere and Payson's good company began to ease Harriet's tension and she found herself relaxing.

She sat back and took a good look at her handsome companion. Payson was a slim man who always managed to look elegantly dressed, even in khaki shorts, an open neck polo shirt, and sandals. His elegance was a quality that came from within. Unlike most people it wasn't something he donned for the public and then took off with his clothing.

Although only seventy-six, Payson had opted not to color his thick, snow white hair and wore it tied back in a short queue. She liked that lack of vanity about him.

Harriet didn't know why Payson had singled her out and befriended her when she first came to the island, but she deeply valued his friendship. Their Thursday lunch dates were something she eagerly looked forward to. Payson had taken on the role of a favorite uncle, something she'd never had.

They talked about inconsequential things until their lunch was served.

"So tell me, Harry, how is your project for the underprivileged children coming along?"

Harriet swallowed a bite of perfectly grilled sweet sea scallop and set down her fork. For the last two months she had been working on a way to bring groups of underprivileged children to the resort for a week's stay. The key had been to find corporate and private sponsors to cover the costs so it didn't come out of the resort's profits.

"Finding sponsors was easier than I had expected," she told Payson enthusiastically. "The first group of kids arrives next Saturday. I found two businesses to foot the bills for their air shuttles, rooms, and meals. I figure everything else is already in place here on the island so won't cost any extra. In return for their sponsorship the businesses will be the first names engraved on a big brass plaque I had designed in the shape of the island. It's already hanging in the main lobby."

Payson smiled at her. "Your enthusiasm is wonderful to see. How many children in the first group and what do you have planned for them?"

"Only twenty in this first group. They're my guinea pigs. I want to see if and what problems arise and have workarounds figured out before I bring in any more. After that we'll try to bring in thirty once a month. That way we won't tax the resort staff."

She took a bite of her mango salad, relishing the citric burst of lime blended with the sweet mango. The island food was far more exotic than any she'd eaten back in Maine. She knew what it was to go hungry and she savored every bite.

"As for entertainment," she continued, "I'm going to set up a tour for them their first day here—show them the circus, the amusement park, and the marina.

"Rather than schedule them for everything, I'm thinking I'll show them what's available for them to do and then I'll let them decide for themselves what interests them. These kids have led very limited lives with few opportunities to make their own choices. I think a week of freedom—within limits of course—will be good for them."

She frowned at Payson. "They'll be chaperoned, of course. Please don't worry that they'll cause mischief."

"I expected nothing less. How did you work that out? Are you bringing adults in with the children?"

Harriet shook her head. "No. This first group comes from an inner New York City orphanage. I think they need to get away from their keepers. Albie is going to help me with the tour their first day here."

Albion Aloysius Carter was the head baggage clerk at the resort's hotel. In his sixties, with dark skin, curly gray hair, and an engaging smile, he had also befriended Harriet shortly after her arrival.

"Each department is pitching in," she continued. "The marina has droids to help the kids who want to learn how to sail or kayak, or even learn to swim. The amusement park and circus will assign workers to look after and help the kids while they're there. A few members of the hotel and waitstaff have volunteered to watch over the ones who want to hang on the beach. The only place they won't be able to go is the spa because it's already booked solid."

She gave Payson an anxious look. "Everything will get done for the other guests, I promise. No one will be neglected."

Payson reached across the table and gently squeezed Harriet's hand.

"Finish your lunch. I foresee no issues with the staff helping. It sounds as if you've worked everything out and I suspect everyone—children *and* staff—will enjoy themselves immensely. It was an inspired idea, Harry, and I'm sure it will be a rousing success. Would you like dessert? I have my eye on an orange ice."

They finished their lunch and walked back to Harriet's

office building. She gave Payson a kiss on the cheek, promised to join him for lunch the following week, and headed inside.

It wasn't until she was walking down the hall to her office that she realized Payson had intentionally distracted her from thoughts of finding Arlo's frozen body.

"Clever old man," she muttered.

Heaving a sigh she turned around and headed back outside. She needed to see Chef Fritola and figure out what to do with the ice sculptures.

CHAPTER SIX

She found Chef Fritola overseeing the making of appetizers for the Pelookie party. There was no sign of Alex or Dr. Clarke in the busy kitchen. A piece of bright orange tape lettered with KEEP OUT was plastered over the freezer door.

Trays of tiny mushroom quiches and miniature figs stuffed with goat cheese filled two rolling racks next to the chef. Cajun spiced crab croquettes and caponata bruschetta filled two more.

"The appetizers smell and look delicious, Chef," Harriet told him. She would have dearly loved to try one but knew that it would upset the chef if she messed with his neatly ordered trays. "Do you have a quick minute?"

Chef looked put upon but he rolled his hand for her to proceed while he continued placing a spiced, minced filling on tiny wrappers and folding them into neatly shaped packages.

"We need to fix the scarlet A on Adelaide Pelookie's bust. Do you have any ideas? Can we scrape it off?"

Chef frowned while he deftly closed and twisted the little

pockets of filling, then set them in tidy rows on an empty tray. The scents of ginger and soy floated up from the large bowl of filling at his elbow.

"If we scrape the letter off we will leave a large depression in the forehead. That will not work."

"Help me out here, Chef. What can we do? We can't have only three busts on the table. Adrian Pelookie commissioned four. She's expecting to see her mother's face on the table."

"Color all of them," said a sous chef who had been eavesdropping from the next table over. 'If you flush the A with water until it fades and then color the whole bust maybe the A won't show."

Harriet turned eagerly to Chef. "Would that work? Maybe we could color them four different colors, make it look like we intended to do that all along."

The Chef grumbled something she couldn't make out. "We could give it a try," he said reluctantly. He looked at the sous chef who had made the suggestion. "You. Go find me four watercolor dyes. Make sure one is red."

"Yes, Chef." The sous chef took off at a run.

Chef Fritola looked at Harriet. "I will deal with it. You may leave now. I need to finish these appetizers."

Harriet suppressed a grin. "Yes, Chef. The appetizers look wonderful by the way."

Chef ignored her compliment. He had dismissed her and she no longer occupied a place in his mind.

Five minutes later Harriet stood outside her office building and wondered what to do next. The food for the party was being handled. A section of the beach had been roped off and tables and seating were being set up that afternoon. Drinks were cooling. The daughter who had organized the family party was providing the music.

For the moment it seemed that there was nothing more

that she could do. Harriet allowed her shoulders to relax slightly.

"Miss Monroe. I need to speak with you."

Harriet suppressed a groan when she turned and recognized the tall, statuesque blonde bearing down on her. Her shoulders immediately tensed again. She had a feeling she knew what Adrian Pelookie wanted to see her about and she really didn't want to discuss it.

She pasted a smile on her face however, and waited for the woman to reach her.

"Miss Pelookie, how can I help you? Everything for your big party is in hand."

Adrian Pelookie stopped in front of Harriet. Although they'd spoken by link many times, this was their first face to face meeting. Adrian was tall for a woman, but at five eleven Harriet topped her. It was obvious to Harriet that Adrian wasn't used to other women looking down on her and Harriet could see that Adrian didn't like it.

Tough cookies. Adrian Pelookie had not been easy to deal with during any of their link conversations. Harriet had found the woman demanding and obnoxious.

"Everything is in hand?" Adrian raised her carefully plucked eyebrows. Dark green eyes bored into Harriet's own. "That's not what I hear, Miss Monroe. Rumor has it that something happened to my mother's ice sculpture. I expect to see it on the table tonight."

Crap. Harriet had hoped that the overbearing daughter of Adelaide and Bennet Pelookie wouldn't hear about the scarlet A. She sighed inwardly. She should know better by now. The resort's gossip chain hit the guests almost as fast as it hit the staff.

"I assure you the issue has been dealt with, Miss Pelookie," she answered evenly. "You needn't worry. There will be four ice sculptures on the center table as requested."

Adrian frowned. "I should hope so. I paid enough for them."

Harriet refrained from pointing out that not one penny of the cost for the party had come out of Adrian's own pocket. The family corporation had paid for everything.

"If there's nothing else I can do for you, Miss Pelookie, I need to get to my office."

But Adrian wasn't ready to let her go. "Are the chairs and tables set up? What about the food I ordered?"

Harriet forced herself to be patient. "The seating area is being set up as we speak. I just came from the kitchen. The food is being prepped. The beverages are chilling. You told me you were bringing the music. You only have to give it to one of the waitstaff and they'll feed it into the sound system."

"Fine. But I'm warning you, I'd better be happy with the ice sculptures or I'll stop payment on everything."

Harriet stared until the other woman flushed. It had been a ridiculous, empty threat and Adrian knew it. The resort had gone above and beyond to meet the family's needs for the past week.

Adrian's eyes glittered with anger and something Harriet couldn't identify.

What an unpleasant, spiteful woman.

"I'm sure you'll be satisfied, Miss Pelookie," Harriet said, careful to keep her tone neutral. "Now if you'll excuse me I have work to do."

CHAPTER SEVEN

Harriet turned away from Adrian and entered her office building. God save her from the Adrian Pelookies of the world. The woman had grown up in the lap of luxury and obviously enjoyed throwing her weight around. She seemed to especially enjoy lording it over the "little people"–those who worked for a living.

"You're back! I thought you had left for the day. Oh dear." Jeeves looked pained. "A Richard Pelookie stopped by to see you and I told him you were gone for the day."

Harriet had to think for a minute to remember which brother Richard was. There were three Pelookie bothers–Bennet, Samuel, and Richard. Richard was the middle brother. She hadn't spoken with him yet and wondered why he wanted to see her.

"No worries. I'll tag him on the link from my office, Jeeves. I'm sure it was nothing too important."

It took Harriet a few minutes to search her files and find a link number for Richard. The man who answered the call was dark haired and square jawed and definitely a Pelookie.

Hopefully he would turn out to be more pleasant to deal with than Adrian.

"Mr. Pelookie? This is Harriet Monroe. I'm told you wanted to speak with me."

"Yes. But not over the link. Can we meet somewhere?"

Puzzled but not alarmed, Harriet agreed to meet Richard on the beach in front of the hotel in ten minutes. She decided to take her knapsack and head straight home after she spoke with Richard. Since she had to monitor the party that night it was going to be a long work day and she could use a quick refresher nap.

She removed her shoes to walk barefoot in the sand despite the fact that she was meeting with a guest. The fine sand was warm and slightly abrasive on her feet until she hit the firmer, cooler, wetter sand below the tide line. She twisted her feet slightly as she walked, reveling in the slight burn it produced in her calf muscles.

"Thank you for meeting me," Richard said as he joined her. "This must seem a bit cloak and dagger but I didn't want to risk being overheard."

Harriet inspected the man. He was a decade older than he looked, late sixties according to his company bio, and obviously took good care of himself. Either that or he availed himself of the latest body-sculpting and surgeries that took the telltale signs of age off one's face and body.

Dressed in blue and green-checked board shorts and a dark blue tee shirt, she could see that Richard was fit and tanned. Too tanned for a man who spent hours in a gym. She figured Richard's color came from hours on a tennis court or golf course.

Dark brown eyes assessed her in return.

"What can I do for you, Mr. Pelookie?" Harriet asked, uncomfortable under his scrutiny.

"Richie, please. Or Richard, if Richie is too informal for you." He smiled and Harriet could see that the man possessed some charm and was used to employing it.

"I want to know what happened to Adelaide's ice sculpture. Before you deny it, I should tell you that I overheard Adrian say something about a scarlet A on Adelaide's forehead."

"I really don't know any more than that, Mr. Pelookie. But I can assure you that the ice sculpture is not ruined."

She cocked her head and looked at him. "I was under the impression that the ice sculptures were supposed to be a surprise. Does everyone know about them?"

"Please." Richard gave Harriet a disgusted look. "Adrian couldn't keep a secret if her life depended on it. Especially if it makes her look good. She wants everyone to know how wonderful she was to think of having them made. My niece could drive anyone batshit crazy with her constant need for public approval, if you want to know the truth."

Harriet suppressed a grin at the man's candor about his niece. "So the great reveal tonight won't be so great after all."

Richard shrugged one shoulder dismissively. Apparently Adrian's big event meant little or nothing to him.

"So why do you think someone put a big red A on Adelaide's bust? Is it just A for Adelaide?"

Richard looked out over the water for a long moment. "Do you know the story of the Scarlet Letter?" he finally asked, turning back toward Harriet.

"No. I don't think I do."

"Nathaniel Hawthorne wrote it in 1850. It's the story of a young Puritan widow in 1650's Massachusetts who had an affair and was found out because she got pregnant. She was forced to wear a large scarlet A sewn to her chest so everyone would know she was an adulteress and that they should shun her as was proper at the time."

Harriet frowned at him. "Are you saying that someone put the scarlet A on Adelaide's bust because they think she's an adulteress?"

Richard's dark eyes held a hint of sadness. "There were rumors once, but that was decades ago. Addy was a very . . . popular woman when she was younger. But why would someone want to publicize that now? Besides, these aren't puritanical times, are they? Sex is much more in the open and freer."

Harriet didn't know what to say. She felt uncomfortable hearing about the Pelookie family's dirty laundry. Adelaide Pelookie was a beautiful woman. It wouldn't surprise her to learn that she had had lovers when she was younger.

But that wouldn't make her an adulteress, Harriet realized. Had she taken lovers after her marriage to Bennet Pelookie? It wasn't a question she could ask. Or even wanted to ask.

"Do you have any idea who put the A on Adelaide's bust, Mr. Pelookie? If you do, you should talk to the resort's security director, Alex Hayes."

If the Pelookie family knew about the ruined bust they must have also heard about Arlo, yet neither Adrian nor Richard had shown any concern for the death of a lowly kitchen worker. A slow boil of anger began to burn in Harriet's belly.

"You must have also heard that one of the kitchen workers was found in the freezer this morning near the busts. Frozen to death."

"I heard." Richard shook his head. "Nothing to do with us, I'm sure. Idiot must have gotten himself locked in." He narrowed his eyes at Harriet. "Unless you're saying the kitchen worker ruined the bust?"

"I can't think of any reason why Arlo would do that, Mr. Pelookie, can you?"

"Thank you for speaking with me, Miss Monroe." Richard Pelookie turned and walked back toward the hotel where his family was staying without answering Harriet's question.

Harriet watched the man disappear. The conversation had left her feeling unsettled and angry. She decided to delay her nap a little longer and go speak to Alex instead.

There could be something in Richard's story about the scarlet letter that would help him figure out why Chef's nephew Arlo had been trapped in a freezer and left to freeze to death.

Was the scarlet A the work of Arlo? It seemed likely since he was found near the busts. If it was, why did he choose that particular bust and why the letter A? It made no sense unless someone put him up to it. That someone would have to be a Pelookie family member.

She sighed. There were nearly thirty adult Pelookies staying at the resort which gave them far too many suspects.

Alex's greeter droid Mary told her Alex was out of his office so Harriet reversed course and headed back to her cottage. Walking the narrow pink crushed shell road that ran the length of the island's shoreline helped her regain her good spirits.

The Pelookie problems would sort themselves out, and Alex and Tarbell would eventually find Arlo's killer.

A pod of blue-gray dolphins carved an arc above the waves and disappeared, scattering prisms of light. Snow white gulls with black heads wheeled over her head, shattering the peaceful afternoon with their raucous cries.

A painting of a mermaid sitting on a rock over her front door looked down on Harriet as she let herself into Mermaid Cottage. She deactivated the alarm, kicked off her shoes, and dropped her backpack on the floor, then headed straight to the bedroom.

The bedroom and living room of her cottage were

paneled in soothing red-brown mahogany. Thick, woven grass mats cushioned the bamboo floors and comfortable padded furniture invited sitting. It was a cottage fit for the wealthy class, a class she definitely did not belong to.

She blessed every day she lived there.

She looked with longing at the king size bed surrounded by filmy white mosquito netting but decided to shower before her nap. The morning's events had left her feeling tainted and slightly grungy and she didn't want to bring that to bed with her.

The square cottage had only four rooms: the bedroom, living room, a deluxe kitchen, and an even nicer bathroom. Of the four, the bathroom was Harriet's favorite. The mahogany wood had been carried into the bathroom but only on the lower walls and as an accent. The floor and upper walls were a pale, creamy marble tile shot through with rust-colored veins that matched the mahogany trim and vanity.

The vaulted ceiling curved above her, covered with one inch mosaic tiles depicting a mermaid sitting on a rock surrounded by the sea–a much larger and more intricate version of the plaque over the cottage's front door.

A glass walled shower large enough to hold several people filled one corner of the space and a free standing slipper tub sat in front of a pair of carved wooden doors that opened to a deep, covered lanai and the ocean breezes.

Since she didn't have time for a soak Harriet opted for a steam shower, after which she wrapped herself in a fluffy robe and crawled between the sheets of her bed where she promptly fell into a dreamless sleep.

A knock on the bedroom's glass doors that opened onto the wraparound lanai woke her.

"Harry! Wake up."

Harriet reluctantly lifted her head, saw who it was, and buried her face in the pillow.

"Go away. I need my beauty sleep."

"You're beautiful enough already. Let me in. I heard you found another body."

Harriet groaned but dragged herself from the bed and unlocked the lanai doors. "Sol. Why didn't you use your key?"

Solomon Ayers lived in Venus, the cottage next to Mermaid. He had been Harriet's closest and dearest friend since they'd met up on the streets of Portland, Maine when both were young teen runaways.

"I never expected to find you sleeping in the middle of the day." Solly looked at her with concern. "You *never* take naps, Harry–not unless you're ill. What's up? And before you answer that tell me about the body you found this morning."

"Ghoul. Make me some coffee while I get dressed. I'll be right out."

Harriet contemplated the what-to-wear decision for a long minute, then chose a pair of slim capris in deep blue and paired them with a pale gold tank top and her favorite beaded belt. She needed to dress better than the event wait-staff but not as nice as the guests. Checking herself in the full length mirror she decided she had hit the target.

She joined Solly in the cottage's high end kitchen and took a padded stool at the rose granite island, inhaling the smell of ground coffee beans while she watched her friend make a pot of the precious bean juice.

After half a cup of strong black coffee she began to relate the day's events to Solly. He listened closely without interruption, like he always did. His listening skills were one of the traits she most admired about her friend.

"Poor Arlo." Solly sipped his water. He rarely drank coffee after breakfast because it kept him up at night. "I wonder why he was in the freezer. And if Chef had to unlock it with a code how did Arlo get in there in the first place? And who sabotaged the door so he couldn't get out? Sounds fishy, Harry. Poor kid," he repeated.

"All good questions, Sol. I'm sure Alex is talking to everyone he can. What did you think of Richard Pelookie's story about the scarlet A and his comment about old rumors? It felt a little weird at the time. If he already knew about the A why come looking for me? And why tell me that story?"

Solly refilled Harriet's coffee cup. She sniffed appreciatively. The hot dark brew tasted nutty and slightly bitter and smelled heavenly. She could already feel the caffeine waking her up.

Before taking the resort job she could count the number of times she'd been able to afford real coffee on one hand. Now she indulged in a pot every day. Yet another thing to thank Douglas Wade for when she finally got to meet the man.

"I admit that Richard's conversation sounds a little weird," Solly said slowly. "But maybe he's the kind of guy who has to verify rumors. Those business tycoon types can be like that."

"But telling me the story about the Scarlet Letter sounds like he's trying to *start* rumors," Harriet pointed out. "And he as much as said that Adelaide Pelookie was an adulteress. His question was why is someone making a stink about it now?"

Solly set his empty glass down and headed for the door.

"Hey! Where are you going? I thought we were talking."

"To get dressed. I'm coming with you to the party. You might need me. If anyone asks I'm there to check on the all the flower arrangements." The front door slammed.

Harriet finished her coffee and mulled over the day. It had started out strange and kept getting stranger. The highlight had been her lunch with Payson. Payson had assured her that Douglas Wade would not fire her despite her propensity for finding bodies.

She shuddered at the remembered image of poor frozen Arlo.

She sent up a prayer that this would be the last one.

CHAPTER EIGHT

Solly returned to Harriet's door twenty minutes later looking very smart in stone khakis and a sage green button-down shirt that set off his tanned face and the sun-kissed highlights in his brown hair.

Solly was one of the most handsome men Harriet had ever met and he constantly turned heads.

Unfortunately for the women who lusted after him, her closest friend preferred to carry on his love affairs with men.

"You look great," she told him as she set the cottage security system.

"So do you." He smiled and held out his hand. "Island life agrees with you."

Harriet linked her hand with his and they set off toward the main resort. "You have to admit that we've come a long way from the days when we spent freezing winter nights huddled in doorways to get out of the wind."

Solly grinned at her. "Or when we stood over sewer grates because they were the warmest spots we could find."

Harriet wrinkled her nose at the memory. "Warmest *and* smelliest. Let's talk about something more pleasant."

"Okay. Is your hottie going to be at the Pelookie party tonight?"

She had given up on getting Solly to quit referring to Alex as *her hottie*. In truth, she couldn't argue with him. Alex *was* a hottie. And for reasons she still didn't understand he seemed to be serious about her.

"I don't know. Alex is probably busy investigating Arlo's death. Plus he has no reason to be at the party."

She was pleasantly surprised and excited to learn upon their arrival that she was wrong. Alex was indeed attending the Pelookie party. He approached her and Solly as soon as they arrived.

"Just keeping an eye on things," he told them. "After the trouble over the ice sculptures I thought maybe I'd better be handy in case something else happens."

Adrian Pelookie approached them on skinny high heels ill suited for walking in the sand. She wore a shiny silver dress that plunged to her navel and hugged her curves. Her blonde hair was piled high on top of her head exposing a long, slim neck. Diamonds caught the light and shimmered around her neck and wrist and dangled from her ears to her shoulders.

Harriet idly wondered how Adrian kept her breasts from falling out of the revealing dress. The outfit looked a little over the top for the island, but she shouldn't judge–Adrian might have felt the need to dress for her big moment.

"It looks like your party is a success," Harriet told her when Adrian stopped next to them.

"*Event*, Miss Monroe. I've corrected you several times now. This is not a party, it is an *event*."

Harriet knew Adrian hadn't corrected her. She also knew better than to argue with a guest. She pasted on a smile.

"Of course. I stand corrected. Your family appears to be enjoying themselves at your *event*. Kudos to you for organizing it."

"Yes, well they haven't seen the big reveal yet." Adrian dismissed Harriet and turned to Alex. Her voice turned positively husky.

"Why haven't we been introduced?" She laid a hand on Alex's chest.

Harriet thought she actually heard the woman purr. She narrowed her eyes at Adrian.

"I'm sure I would have noticed such a fine looking man if I had seen you around the resort. Have you just arrived? I may have to extend my stay."

Alex removed Adrian's hand from his chest. "Miss Pelookie, I see that you've met my girlfriend, Harriet Monroe. This is our friend, Solomon Ayers."

Adrian cast a quick glance at Solly and dismissed him. "Oh, there's Richard. I need to speak with him." She wobbled off on her ridiculous shoes.

"Well," said Solly, "I'd feel insulted except that she definitely isn't my type. Thanks for trying to fob her off on me, pal. I owe you one." The two men grinned at each other.

"I'm going to check on the flower arrangements. I'll catch up with you two later." Solly kissed Harriet's cheek and disappeared into the milling Pelookie family.

"I was looking for you earlier," Harriet said, turning to Alex once they were alone. "Richard Pelookie tracked me down this afternoon."

"Yeah? What did he want?" Alex placed a large, warm hand on the small of Harriet's back and guided her to a couple of empty chairs near the dance floor.

Pale yellow faerie lights that wound around the smooth palm trunks and through their drooping fronds twinkled around the edges of the setup.

Harriet noted with approval that the raised wooden dance floor, surrounded with seating, had been erected off to one side with the long tables of food off to the other. The sand in between was filled with the elegantly dressed Pelookie adults and children.

Music played softly in the background. She couldn't make out the song over the din of many voices. The soft night breeze carried a blend of expensive perfumes and colognes mixed with the salty brine of beached seaweed.

They took seats facing the crowd. Harriet was intensely aware of Alex sitting next to her, as if every cell in her body had snapped to attention and was reaching for him. He'd had this effect on her from their first meeting and she still wasn't used to it. Somehow Alex made her feel more alive.

"So, what did Richard Pelookie want?" he asked, breaking into her thoughts.

"He asked me about the red A on Adelaide's bust and told me a story from the 1800s called the Scarlet Letter. Do you know it?" She related the tale to Alex while he listened carefully, his eyes never leaving the crowd.

When she'd finished he picked up her hand and turned it to press his lips gently to her palm, then laced her fingers with his.

"You look beautiful tonight," he told her.

Harriet swore that her heart skipped a beat whenever Alex turned his insanely dark blue eyes on her. Eyes that seemed to see everything and miss nothing. She looked into those eyes now and felt her pulse quicken.

"Thank you." She smiled. "So do you." Neither the scar slicing through his right eyebrow nor his slightly crooked nose took away from Alex's rugged good looks. If anything they added to his aura of alpha male. In Harriet's eyes Alex Hayes was the most incredibly sexy man she'd ever met.

Alex chuckled at her compliment, the dimple in his right cheek showing briefly. He leaned toward her and kissed her lightly on the lips. When he settled back in his seat all the playfulness had left his face.

"Fox and I agree that Arlo was murdered," he said quietly so no one could overhear. "There's no way his being trapped in the freezer could be an accident. Not with the way the freezer door had been tampered with and Arlo's missing shoes. I talked to the kitchen staff and no one saw him enter the freezer. Several mentioned seeing him leave the kitchen after his shift ended yesterday. One sous chef said Arlo seemed unusually pleased about something but Arlo didn't give him any details as to why."

"Chef said Arlo had only been here a few weeks," Harriet pointed out. "Is it possible that he had already made an enemy?"

Alex shook his head. "Not from what I heard. Everyone seemed to like him. He was described as harmless, pleasant, immature, and eager to please. Always willing to help out where needed. I didn't pick up any wrong notes so I'm inclined to believe everyone's assessment."

The music stopped and Adrian Pelookie's voice could be heard urging everyone to gather around the center table.

"Shall we?" Alex stood and pulled Harriet to her feet. They wandered over to stand in the shadows at the back edge of the crowd.

CHAPTER NINE

Adrian stood alone behind the center table facing her extended family. She looked edgy and excited.

Alex slid an arm around Harriet's waist and she leaned into him. She caught sight of Solly leaning against a palm in the shadows behind Adrian.

Adelaide and Bennet Pelookie stood at the center front of the crowd near the table. Samuel Pelookie stood next to Bennet with a pretty redhead at his side. Richard stood with a blonde woman Harriet assumed was his wife on their other side.

The three brothers and Adelaide, the cornerstones of the Pelookie empire.

A red silk cloth covered the bulky shapes on the table in front of Adrian. A dozen candles in clear glass holders cast flickering shadows onto the cloth.

Harriet knew the busts were about to be revealed and held her breath, anxious to see how well Chef had dealt with the bothersome red A. She tuned back into Adrian's speech.

"And so, in honor of our company's founding four members—my mother Adelaide, my father Bennet, uncles

Richard and Samuel Pelookie–and the fact that they've steered Pelookie Prisons into its best year ever, larger than life bronze replicas of these busts will be placed in the lobby of Pelookie headquarters."

Adrian whipped off the cloth to a polite smattering of applause.

Harriet was pleased to see that Chef had done a marvelous job of disguising the red A.

Bennet's and Adelaide's busts sat in the center. They had been colored completely in red, Richard's in blue, and Samuel's in green. The colors were deep but not opaque, and the flickering candle lights shone through and reflected off the ice.

Adrian was staring at the crowd, not the busts, when she whipped off the concealing cloth. Harriet watched her expression go from one of anticipation to puzzlement. When she finally glanced down at the four ice sculptures puzzlement changed to anger.

"Chef did a good job hiding the A," Alex said quietly. "Good. I was afraid there would be some high drama. From her expression, it appears that Adrian was hoping for a bigger reaction."

They turned and began to walk away from the Pelookie crowd.

Someone turned up the volume on the music. Old-fashioned rock and roll blared from the speakers hidden under the edges of the raised dance floor. Couples stepped up and began to dance.

Harriet glanced over her shoulder and saw Adrian still staring at the busts. Anger and something ugly marred the woman's pretty face.

It seemed obvious to Harriet from Adrian's expression that she had wanted the red A to be noticed. The question was, why?

Adrian looked up at that moment and caught Harriet watching her. She flipped Harriet a rude gesture and scowled before turning away and stomping off toward the dark jungle growth beyond the edges of the party.

"I need to check with the waitstaff and make sure the food and drinks are doing okay," Harriet told Alex. "Will you be sticking around?"

"I'll come with you. I could use a bite to eat. I missed lunch and dinner today."

They walked to the end of the row of tables where the waitstaff was replenishing empty trays with appetizers and grabbed a few to sample.

"Mmmm. These potsticker thingies are good," Alex said, popping a second one into his mouth. "Try one." He held the appetizer to Harriet's lips.

"Mmm, you're right. Delish. Try one of the cajun crab croquettes. They're one of Chef's specialties." Harriet popped a croquette into her mouth and chewed happily. Before she could eat a second one she thought she heard a woman shout. The sound cut off abruptly so she couldn't be sure.

She turned to look at the party but no one seemed upset. The music continued to play and dancers young and old gyrated their bodies on the wooden dance floor and in the surrounding sand. Waitstaff circulated with trays filled with the delicious appetizers and collected empty drink glasses and used plates and napkins.

"Did you hear someone shout?" Harriet turned back toward Alex, but he was already moving toward the sound. The shout had come from the same direction Adrian had taken when she stormed off, Harriet realized.

The woman had most likely twisted her ankle stomping through the sand in her ridiculous stiletto heels. She hurried after Alex in case he needed her help getting Adrian to a chair.

The island grew inky dark once they were away from the artificial lights surrounding the party, making it hard for Harriet to see where she was walking. Fortunately a half moon shed a faint light so she wasn't completely blind.

She stopped to slip off her wedge sandals so she could walk faster without risking her own turned ankle. Without the sun beating on it the temperature of the sand had dropped and it felt almost cold on Harriet's bare feet.

"Alex?"

"Over here." A light blinked off and on near the trees to her left.

Harriet veered toward the light. "Is it Adrian? Is she hurt?"

"Don't come any closer."

"Why not?" Alex's flashlight blinked on and caught a sparkle of silver on the ground.

"Has she sprained her ankle?" Even as she asked the question her intuition gave her the answer.

"No."

Harriet swallowed the lump that suddenly swelled in her throat. "Oh, no," she whispered. "That's Adrian Pelookie on the ground. She's dead, isn't she?"

"The answer is yes. Yes, that's Adrian. Yes, she's dead." Alex's voice sounded cold and furious. He fished his link from his back pocket.

"Fox. I need you to pick up Dr. Clarke and meet me on the north side of the main hotel. Bring a body bag and a stretcher." He listened for a minute. "Definitely murder. I'll meet you behind the hotel and guide you to the body."

"Murder?" Harriet forced herself to take a deep breath.

"Harry? Alex? What can I do?" Solly appeared at Harriet's side and put an arm around her shoulder. "I saw you two rush away from the party. And I just overheard Harry say murder just now. Who is it?"

"Adrian Pelookie. I need you and Harriet to stay here with the body while I meet Fox and the doc. Don't get any closer. Don't let anybody come near. I haven't had a chance to look for footprints or anything else that her killer might have left behind."

Harriet knew there wouldn't be any clear footprints in the soft sand but she had no desire to get any closer to the body.

"We'll wait," Solly said quietly.

CHAPTER TEN

The wait for Alex to return with Fox and Dr. Clarke felt interminable to Harriet. Some poor creature screeched in the dark jungle beyond the hotel grounds, sending a shiver up her back.

Another death. This one most likely a meal for something higher up the food chain.

The family party continued on behind them, oblivious to the lifeless body of Adrian Pelookie lying in the cooling sand less than a hundred feet away. Laughter and conversation underscored the music which had been turned down to a more reasonable level.

Harriet wondered if one of the waitstaff had turned down the volume so the party wouldn't bother the resort's other guests staying in the hotel. That made her wonder who had turned the music up in the first place. Had the killer used the loud rock and roll to cover any sound Adrian might make when he attacked her?

"Solly, did you see who switched on the loud music?"

"Nope. I was hoping to snatch a couple of appetizers and was heading toward you and Alex from the other side of the dance floor when I saw Alex run off. You followed Alex so I followed you."

That meant Solly hadn't heard Adrian shout. If he hadn't been able to hear Adrian over the music it stood to reason that none of the other attendees could have heard her either.

"How did you get to the other side of the dance floor? I saw you standing behind Adrian just before her great reveal."

"I was trying to be unobtrusive by hanging back, but I realized if anyone took photos I might get caught in them so I decided to walk around the outside of the party instead of through it since I wasn't a guest."

"Did you see Adrian reveal the ice sculptures?"

"Nope. Missed it. I heard her speech and a few claps. It didn't sound as if the family thought her big surprise was much of a surprise."

"Richard Pelookie told me everyone knew about the ice sculptures because Adrian couldn't keep her surprise a secret."

"That only partially explains the tepid response. Shouldn't they have shown their support for her efforts even if it wasn't a surprise?"

A good question.

Alex returned, leading Fox and Dr. Clarke, before Harriet could reply. Dr. Clarke carried a black, rolled up body bag under one arm. Fox carried a lightweight body board from the beach lifeguards emergency kit. They stopped beside Harriet and Solly.

"The body's just over there. We need to do this discreetly," Alex told them. "I want the body out of here before I shut down the party and start interviewing everyone."

It had already been a day filled with interviews because of the young chef Arlo's murder and Alex was feeling tired and drained. Unfortunately it looked like the night would also be filled with interviews for Adrian's murder.

He had expected to put murder investigations behind him when he quit his job as a homicide detective in the country's largest city to take up the job of security director for the ultra high end Island Resort. The wealthy classes were supposed to be above that sort of thing.

So much for his expectations. This was the resort's fourth suspicious death in three months. Two in one day–he might as well have stayed in New York City. Except that then he wouldn't have met Harriet.

He looked at her worried expression and attempted a smile that felt more like a grimace.

"Are you absolutely certain she was murdered?" Harriet asked. She hated to see how drawn and tired Alex's face looked.

"I'm sorry, Harriet. There's no question about cause of death. Someone bashed in Adrian Pelookie's skull with a coconut. Wait here with Solly while we bag her up, okay?" He led Fox and the doctor to Adrian's body.

Harriet had no desire to see Adrian's lifeless body. Goosebumps rose on her bare arms despite the warm night. She set down her shoes and rubbed her arms in an effort to warm herself.

"I can't believe it, Solly. Another murder. Adrian wasn't an easy person to like but she didn't deserve to be murdered. I know this sounds terribly selfish of me, but I'm glad Alex was the one to find the body this time and not me."

Solly wrapped his arms around her and hugged her to his chest to lend his warmth. "You're not selfish," he told her. "No one can blame you for not wanting to stumble over another body."

He turned slightly so they could watch Alex and the doctor. "If I didn't know better I'd think that people purposely chose the resort to do their dastardly deeds."

"Dastardly deeds," Harriet repeated. "I like that. Good

alliteration. I think I'll work it into the Murder Dinner Theatre spiel." She knew she sounded callous, but if she allowed herself to dwell on dead bodies there was no question but that she'd fall apart.

"Dastardly Deeds at Destination Death," Solly answered. "Has a certain ring to it." His attempt at humor fell flat and they both sighed.

"Do you think the resort will be able to survive this?" She could barely make out her friend's warm brown eyes in the dim light as he looked down at her.

Solly barked out a laugh. "Harry, think about it. This place is only going to become more famous. Everyone will want to stay here in the hopes that they'll be here for a murder and have a tale to tell their friends and family when they get home."

"That's awful."

"No. That's people. We're all ghouls at heart."

Alex and Fox approached them then, supporting the stretcher bearing the body between them with Dr. Clarke following. To Harriet's relief, Adrian Pelookie was completely enclosed in the black body bag.

Dr. Clarke stopped beside Harriet and Solly. "Mr. Ayers. Miss Monroe. Why aren't I surprised to see you here?"

"Luck of the draw, Dr. Clarke," Solly answered dryly.

Dr. Clarke walked on with Harriet and Solly following behind. Fox had parked the resort's larger, more powerful vehicle known as the Road Hog in a dark corner just beyond the arc of lights behind the hotel. The two men slid the stretcher into the rear of the Hog while Dr. Clarke, Harriet, and Solly watched in silence.

Alex peeled off his latex gloves, wiped a hand over his face, and turned toward Harriet and Solly. "Don't go back to the party. Go home and get some sleep, both of you. There's no point in waiting for me. I'll interview you both tomorrow morning."

"I'll see Harry home, Alex," Solly said. "I don't think either of us is needed here any longer, especially if you shut down the party."

"Fancy a drink, Harry?" Solly took Harriet's hand and led her toward the road after the others drove off in the Hog. "Let's go sit on your lanai and share a bottle of wine."

Harriet didn't think the wine would be enough to help her sleep but she didn't want to be alone so she agreed. They circled the hotel and walked by the side entrance just as Adelaide Pelookie stepped through the door. She started to hurry past but stopped and turned.

"I recognize you," she said to Harriet. "You're the woman who helped Adrian set up the family retreat. I was just looking for my daughter. I'm afraid that the others weren't quite as enthusiastic about the busts as she had hoped. Adrian's very sensitive, you know. I thought maybe she had retreated to her room to lick her wounded pride but she isn't there. Have you seen her?"

Harriet thought about the body bag being loaded into the rear of the Road Hog. "No, we haven't see her, Mrs. Pelookie. Maybe she's returned to the party. I'd check there if I was you." Let Alex tell her about Adrian.

"Thank you, dear."

Harriet watched Adrian's mother stride off. Adelaide was a classic beauty, with a wide, clear brow, chiseled cheekbones, and large, expressive hazel eyes–tall and blonde like her daughter but with an even more voluptuous build, She moved with a regal grace that Harriet envied.

"She's a beautiful woman even at her age," Solly noted. "She must have turned lots of heads when she was younger."

"I don't hear the music any longer." Harriet watched Adelaide disappear around the corner of the hotel.

"I'm afraid Adelaide will be in for a terrible shock when she learns that her daughter has been murdered. Poor woman. I hated to lie to her, Solly, but I just couldn't tell her that Adrian is dead. I don't know how Alex did it for all those years, informing families that a loved one had been murdered. How do you face that kind of pain over and over again?"

Solly wrapped an arm about Harriet's waist. "Maybe he faced it by knowing that he'd do his best to find the killer. Let's go have that glass of wine, shall we?"

CHAPTER ELEVEN

It took Alex and Fox three hours to interview the members of the stunned Pelookie family and the resort staff that had worked the party. Alex divided the family into two groups with one group sitting in chairs off to the side and the second group sitting on the edges of the dance floor.

He interviewed the group seated on the dance floor, leading them one by one to a spot far enough away that they wouldn't be overheard, then asked only three questions.

"When and where did you last see Adrian Pelookie?"

"Did you notice anyone leaving the party?"

"Who turned on the dance music after Adrian revealed the sculptures?"

Unfortunately the answers shed no light on Adrian Pelookie's last minutes of life.

Fox's interviews produced the same lack of information. They released the family with a warning not to leave the island until they'd been given permission to go and proceeded to interview the waitstaff with similar results.

"I'm sorry, Alex. No one I spoke to saw anything, no one

knows who turned the music up loud enough to cover any sounds when Adrian was attacked, and the last time anyone remembers seeing Adrian she was standing behind her ice sculptures."

Fox shook his head after sharing his poor results. "A few beat their chops trying to sound like they knew something, but nope. Bust."

"Except that someone knows everything because this wasn't a random murder. Adrian Pelookie wasn't killed by a stranger. Someone we talked to tonight is the killer."

The two men walked over to the center table holding the ice sculptures and stared down at the pools of colored water gathered at their bases. The tropical heat had worked its inevitable magic on the ice, distorting the faces into grotesque expressions worthy of a horror movie.

"Arlo and Adrian's murders are linked," Alex said. He pointed to the remains of Adelaide's bust. "And it has something to do with the scarlet A on Adrian's mother's bust. We need to start digging deeper into Adelaide's life and the lives of the three brothers."

"The family made their fortune building and running private prisons, didn't they?"

Fox thought for a second and then answered his own question. "Yes. I remember now. They specialize in the off-planet prisons for hard core lifers. Concrete cells to hold the scum of the earth that no one ever wants to see again. Maybe Adrian's murder was a revenge killing for someone being held off-planet."

"Yeah. Could be something there. We'll have to check it out. My gut still tells me the scarlet A is important, but we'll look at everything."

The waitstaff had cleared away the remainder of the food and drinks and was almost finished with breaking down the last of the tables. The chairs were stacked and being loaded onto a sand sled to be hauled back to the hotel.

"No clues to see here. Go to bed, Fox. Get some sleep. We'll meet at oh-eight-hundred–" Alex checked his watch. "Six hours from now."

He gestured to the two men waiting to break down the table holding the melted busts. "Go ahead. We're finished here. Thank you for waiting."

Alex waited until everyone had cleared out and Fox had reluctantly left him before returning to the spot where he'd found Adrian's body. The island was quiet now that everyone from the Pelookie event had gone to their rooms and cottages, quiet enough that he could hear the waves lapping at the beach and the gentle breeze rattling the palm fronds.

He took out his small flashlight and searched the ground in a methodical grid but found nothing except the stain where the blood from Adrian's head wound had seeped into the sand.

If this was the city he'd have a team of specialists scouring the vicinity for clues. But it wasn't the city. He'd have to come back in the daylight to see if he missed anything.

Something rustled in the undergrowth and he knew the scent of blood had attracted the jungle's scavengers. The resort might be fancy high end but it had been built on an island that was still ninety percent natural wilderness. Dangerous saltwater crocs lived in the mangrove swamp at the island's southern tip and he wouldn't be surprised to learn that there were still a few large predators in the jungle preserve that covered most of the island.

Unlike the jungle's supposedly uncivilized predators who only killed to eat, human predators killed for greed, jealousy, and anger. In Alex's mind that made humans the uncivilized species. He wondered which of those motives was responsible for the two recent murders.

"Get some sleep, Hayes," he said aloud. Whatever had been lurking in the brush crashed off at the sound of his voice. He clicked off the flashlight and headed back to his apartment with only the setting half moon to guide him.

In a few hours he would pick up the hunt.

A sound woke Alex from a deep, dreamless sleep. He rolled onto his back so he could listen with both ears but made no move to get out of his bed. He slept in the nude, with only a light sheet over his body and the windows open, something he'd come to enjoy after years of either freezing or sweltering in New York.

A quick look at his wrist unit told him he'd only been asleep for two hours. In the old days–the days when he was a rookie cop–two hours would have been a sufficient amount of rest. Ten years later he needed a few more hours of shut eye to bounce back.

A soft knock sounded at the apartment door. That must have been what woke him. The knock sounded almost tentative.

So, not an emergency. And not a Pelookie demanding to know what he was doing about the death of one of their own.

The fact that Alex lived over the security office wasn't general knowledge even among the resort staff, eliminating most of the people on the island.

He heaved himself out of the bed with a heavy sigh, pulled on his jeans to cover his nakedness, and padded into the living room without turning on a light.

"Who's there?"

"Alex? It's Harriet."

"Harriet? What are you doing here?" Even though they'd been an item for the last couple of months Harriet had yet to visit his apartment. They always ended up at her place because it was more private and on the beach. Not to mention more comfortable. Alex's apartment was nearly as stark as his office.

Puzzled by the reason behind the unexpected visit, he opened the door. Harriet stood there, looking embarrassed and unhappy and cuddly as a puppy in a pair of sweat pants and a tee shirt. She hugged herself and looked at him.

"I couldn't sleep." She walked into his open arms. "Can I stay with you for the rest of the night? Please?"

Alex closed and locked the door behind her. Taking her hand he led her back to his bedroom and laid beside her on the bed. He kept his jeans on. If he took them off he knew he wouldn't be able to resist making love to Harriet and they both needed sleep.

"Go to sleep," he told her. "I'm meeting Fox in a couple hours and I need to rest." He wrapped his arm around Harriet's waist and snugged her backside up against his body. They were both asleep within minutes.

"Alex?" Something tickled his cheek. He swatted at it.

"Alex, wake up." This time he opened his eyes and saw Harriet leaning over him, her silver blue eyes staring into his. The tickle came from her long, thick hair brushing his cheek.

Sunlight streamed through the bedroom window, lighting up her golden hair and turning it into a halo.

Harriet smiled at him. "Good morning."

Her husky voice sent little currents of desire through his entire body.

Harriet saw the smolder in Alex's heavy-lidded eyes and almost crawled back into the bed with him. She kissed him lightly on the lips instead.

"Thanks for letting me stay. I'm heading home now. I'll be in my office when you're ready to interview me."

Alex grabbed at her but she slid out of his grasp and was gone, leaving his bedroom feeling surprisingly empty.

He had been biding his time with Harriet while he tried to figure out the best way to deal with the psychological damage her aunt and uncle had inflicted on her, but holding her at arm's length was becoming increasingly difficult.

He wanted Harriet Monroe in his life every day and in his bed each night. Permanently. No more pussyfooting around. He wanted marriage and kids. He wanted a family.

After they solved these two murders he was going to take her to the mainland to see a mental trauma specialist that Payson Douglas had recommended. A specialist he hoped could undo the mental blocks another specialist had installed in her mind nearly twenty years before.

Harriet Monroe needed to remember and deal with the fact that at the age of eight she had witnessed a mass suicide that included everyone she knew, including her parents. He had no idea how learning the truth would affect her, but he knew that she had to face her past.

Hopefully she would still love him after he forced her to relive something so horrendous that newspeople still wrote about the mass suicide on every yearly anniversary.

Since there was nothing he could do about Harriet now, Alex put her out of his mind. It was time to get up and start hunting for a killer.

Alex was out of the shower and half dressed before he realized he could smell coffee from the kitchen. Had Harriet come back?

"Harriet?"

Still barefoot, Alex hurried into the kitchen, threading his belt through his pant loops while he walked. He found the kitchen empty, but there was a pot of fresh, hot coffee with a note propped against a waiting travel mug.

Thought you might need this. I love you. H.

Yeah, this woman was definitely a keeper. A deep satisfaction filled Alex.

He filled the mug, shut off the coffee maker and walked downstairs to his office with a smile on his face.

CHAPTER TWELVE

Alex's feeling of contentment lasted for less time than it took him to drink his mug of coffee. As soon as he entered his office lobby he saw Bennet Pelookie waiting in one of the comfortably cushioned, blue and green striped chairs that lined the front wall of the security office.

The colorful chairs, gleaming bamboo floors, green plants, and hot and cold beverage counter made the lobby of the security office look more like a hotel lobby than a police station. It was designed to put the wealthy at ease even when they had crossed the line that was the law.

He might not be a policeman any longer, but on the resort island Alex was the law.

Alex nodded to Bennet and told him he'd be with him in a minute, then walked behind the waist high mahogany counter to speak with his droid, Mary. Built like a fireplug–stocky and sturdy–Mary wore a uniform of khakis and a short sleeved polo in the resort-blue that showed off her muscular build.

Impervious to pain, Mary was stronger than any human

and programmed in most forms of hand to hand combat known to man.

Two frown lines had been created between her eyebrows, intended to give her a serious look. As far as Alex was concerned they were unnecessary. Mary's short black hair, pug nose, and businesslike demeanor made her serious enough. After nearly four months he had yet to see her smile.

"Good morning, Mary. Have you anything to report?"

"Good morning, sir. Mr. Bennet Pelookie would like a word with the person investigating his daughter's death. Tarbell Fox called . . ."

She checked her internal time keeper . . . "Tarbell Fox called four minutes ago and said he'd arrive at the office in ten minutes. That would be six minutes until his arrival now, sir."

"Very good."

"Also, Dr. Clarke called and verified that based on more than one head wound Adrian Pelookie was definitely murdered."

"Ah." Alex hadn't held out much hope that the head wound that killed Adrian had been an accident. That's why he had questioned the party goers last night. But he *had* hoped a little.

It had been known to happen—several dozen people had been killed by falling coconuts over the last two centuries. Unfortunately Adrian Pelookie was not one of them.

"Anything else I should know?"

"Yes, sir. Mr. Payson Douglas asks that you swing by his cottage later today, whenever you get a free moment. He did not designate a time however, sir."

Alex could tell by Mary's voice that she did not approve of appointments made without firm times. Despite the manufacturers claims that droids were emotionless workers, Alex had found that the higher quality droids had slight idiosyncrasies that differentiated them from one another. They might not be human, but they weren't mindless robots either.

"Thank you, Mary. I'll take Mr. Pelookie into Interview Room One now. Tell Mr. Fox to join us as soon as he comes in, will you please?"

Alex refilled his travel mug from the refreshment center coffee pot and took a sip while he studied Bennet Pelookie.

The man looked tired but composed. That was understandable. Bennet had been one of the last family members to be interviewed and had been detained into the wee hours of the morning.

Dark circles bruised the skin beneath Bennet's brown eyes a dusky purple. The brother had the prominent beaked nose that marked all the brothers. His dark hair was liberally salted with silver.

The skin beneath Bennet's chin sagged slightly, one of the few signs that the eldest Pelookie brother was getting on in years. Alex wondered why he hadn't gone for a rejuvenation package like most wealthy older men and women did. A tuck of loose skin, a little body reshaping, and a decade or more disappeared. At least on the outside.

He had to admit that he admired a man who was comfortable enough in his own skin to let the world see it naturally age. He took another sip of the hot, bitter brew and stifled a sigh. It was time to find out why Bennet Pelookie was waiting to speak with him.

Alex stepped forward and extended a hand. "Mr. Pelookie, Alex Hayes, security director. I believe you spoke with my associate, Tarbell Fox, last night. What can I do for you?"

Bennet Pelookie stood. He was not a particularly tall man and had to crane his neck to look up to Alex's six foot four.

"I'd like to see my daughter, Mr. Hayes. I asked around after I left you last night and no one from the immediate family identified the body. How do I know it's really Adrian and not some other guest?"

Despite the belligerent tone Alex took no offense. The unexpected death of a loved one hit people in a thousand different ways.

"I know what your daughter looks like, Mr. Pelookie," he said gently. "I identified her myself. If you wish to see your daughter's body however, that can be arranged."

Bennet Pelookie's shoulders visibly slumped. He rubbed his forehead with the fingers of his left hand. "Sorry. I was hoping . . ." His voice trailed off.

"Why don't we go sit in one of the conference rooms where it's more private? Can I bring you a cup of coffee or an iced fruit drink?"

"A lemonade if you please."

Fox strode through the door in time to catch Bennet's answer. "I'll get it." He scooped ice into a tall glass, topped it with lemonade, and grabbed a hot coffee for himself.

"What's up?" he asked, handing the cold drink to the guest.

"Mr. Pelookie and I were just headed to a conference room to talk. Join us." It wasn't an invitation that could be refused. Alex wanted Fox there when he talked to Bennet. Fox had good instincts and two people making observations were bound to catch more than one person.

Alex waited for Adrian's father to settle before he took his own seat. The conference rooms were a far cry from the interview rooms he'd used as an NYC detective. The room held thick cushioned chairs covered in a bright floral pattern and set around a polished steel-topped table.

A drinks trolley at the far end of the room held soft drinks, water, china cups, and a coffee pot, currently empty. A large window looked out onto the jungle and several landscapes of the island painted by local artists hung on the wall.

"Mr. Pelookie," Alex began.

"Bennet, please. There are three Mr. Pelookies. It cuts down on the confusion when people address us by our first names."

"Very well. Bennet, do you know if your daughter had any enemies?"

"Why would you ask that?" His thick, dark brows met over his eyes. Suddenly they widened. "I thought Adrian's death was an accident–I was told that a coconut fell and hit her in the head."

"Last night that was still a possibility. But I've received word from the resort's doctor that Adrian suffered several blows despite the fact that there was only one coconut lying next to her body."

Bennet flinched when Alex said "body".

"Someone killed my daughter? Why? Adrian could be difficult but she never harmed anyone. I don't understand."

Alex studied the man over the rim of his travel mug. Bennet's reaction seemed sincere.

"Was there anyone who found Adrian particularly difficult?" he asked. "Someone she might have angered recently, perhaps?"

Bennet shook his head. "Not to my knowledge. As I said, Adrian could be difficult when she chose to be. Like the rest of us Pelookies she had strong opinions about things. Her mother and I brought her up to believe in herself and to stand up for whatever she believed in."

Alex decided to try another tack. "Is there anything going on with the family business right now that might have created friction between Adrian and another member of the family?"

Bennet was shaking his head no before Alex finished asking the question. "Definitely not. We've just signed a deal to construct two more off-planet prisons. Everyone voted in favor of the expansion."

He settled into his chair, obviously more comfortable now that they were talking about the business. "The Pelookie family is growing which means more mouths to feed. The two new prisons will boost our bottom line. Everyone wants the project."

Alex looked at Fox and raised one eyebrow. "Do you have any questions, Fox?"

"A couple, if you don't mind. Did Adrian have a special boyfriend, Mr. Pelookie?"

Bennet blinked. A flush crept up his neck. "Adrian was a modern young woman. She liked variety. She dated a lot of men. To my knowledge there was no one in particular." He pressed his lips together in a thin line.

"I take it you didn't approve of her dating practices?"

Alex watched Bennet with interest. The man was obviously uncomfortable talking about his daughter's love life. To be honest he supposed he would feel the same way about his own daughter. When and if he ever had any.

"No. I didn't approve. Are we done here?"

"Almost," Fox drummed his gingers on the tabletop. "How did Adrian's mother . . . Adelaide is it? How did Adelaide feel about Adrian's dating practices–are we talking five men? A dozen men? Fifty? More?"

Bennet stood. "I don't know what Adrian's dating has to do with her murder," he said coldly. "Rather than asking these prurient questions you should be out looking for whoever killed my daughter. If there's nothing else, I'm leaving now."

Alex looked at Fox who gave a slight shake of the head. They were done. "I'll walk you out."

When Alex returned to the conference room he found Fox scowling and tapping the tabletop with his fingers.

"Something there," Fox said. "The father did not approve of Adrian's personal life. It sounds as if she was into weaving the four F's."

Alex furrowed his eyebrows. "I hate when you don't speak English. What are the four F's?"

"Find 'em, fool 'em, frig 'em, and forget 'em. Someone Adrian Pelookie dated might not have appreciated being blown off."

Alex considered Fox's theory, that one of Adrian's rejected lovers had killed her and shook his head.

"I don't think so. The rejected lover just happens to be here on the island? Why would he be invited to the Pelookie celebration?"

"Maybe he crashed it."

"Let's hope not or we might never learn who killed Adrian Pelookie. Just in case, I'll check the resort's list of current guests."

Alex told Fox about the way Adrian had come on to him before the family event despite the fact that Harriet was standing right there.

"Exactly! Adrian seems to have had no boundaries. What if she flirted with another man, one with a jealous spouse or girlfriend? Jealousy is a prime motive for murder."

Fox began to pace the room. He stopped and stood at the window for a long moment. Alex didn't interrupt, giving him space to think. Fox turned from the window.

"Okay, here's another theory. Daddy was embarrassed by his daughter's lifestyle and finally blew his top, decided to do something about it. Maybe she said something to him at the family gig that set him off."

Alex shook his head and scowled. "There's too many theories and not enough data. The bottom line is we have no idea who killed Adrian and why. I'll put together a list and we'll split it up, start re-interviewing everyone at the celebration last night. We can eliminate the kids at least. Adrian was a tall woman and none of them are tall enough to hit her on the head.

"We don't want to forget about Arlo either. Are the two murders connected? Do they have anything to do with the scarlet A on Adelaide Pelookie's bust?"

Fox walked to the door and held it open for Alex. "I hate that people are dead before their time, but I have to confess that I enjoy solving the puzzle of why and who."

"I'll get that list."

Alex left the conference room. Deep down, he could admit that he loved solving the puzzle too. It was the one quality above all others that made a good homicide detective, and he had been the city's top murder cop before he burned out on too many senseless killings.

He had every confidence that he and Fox would find the killer or killers.

The hunt was on.

CHAPTER THIRTEEN

Alex put together his list of potential suspects, dividing them into groups of most likely to least likely. The names could shift on the list as they learned more about the people involved, but he had to start somewhere.

He gave Fox half the names and sent him to track down Solomon Hayes and get his statement about the previous night. While he didn't expect Solly to add much he knew Harriet's friend was observant and not afraid to speak his mind.

Solly had worked with them to solve a suspicious death two months before. In a very loose, unofficial sense, while the gardener/landscape artist did not work for the security department, he had become part of Alex's team. Just as Harriet had.

Alex took his time strolling over to Harriet's office. It was another beautiful day in paradise with the salty smell of the sea riding a soft onshore breeze that lifted the hair off the back of his neck and made him glad he had abandoned the city.

He didn't think he'd ever grow tired of living on the

island. He might get tired of the problems the resort guests could, and did, create, but he'd never tire of the island itself.

Especially now that Harriet lived there. She added a new, exciting dimension to his life that he had thought he'd never experience. He had dated many women while living on the mainland but had grown weary of shallow relationships that went nowhere.

Until Harriet's arrival he had abstained from dating any of the resort's staff even though several of the women had indicated their interest.

Thinking about Harriet put a spring in Alex's step and he was soon greeting Jeeves, Harriet's office reception droid.

Jeeves wore an oatmeal colored linen suit with the resort's signature blue shirt. A neatly folded matching hankie peeked from his left breast pocket. To Alex's eye, Jeeves looked a bit like a dandy. He certainly looked very different from Alex's own droid Mary.

"Good morning, Jeeves. You're looking quite spiffy today."

Jeeves blanked for a moment while he accessed his internal dictionary. "Spiffy? I don't know *spiffy*, sir."

"It means smart. Well put together. You look well put together today, Jeeves. Spiffy."

"Ahhh, thank you, Mr. Hayes. You are looking quite spiffy yourself." He spoke the word carefully. Alex knew that spiffy would remain in Jeeves's databanks forever. Droids really were quite wonderful that way. They never forgot a thing.

"I'm here to see Miss Monroe."

"Yessir. I'm to show you right through."

Alex enjoyed the cool walk down the corridor that led to Harriet's office. Paddle fans turned lazily over his head. Tinted windows looked out on the pink crushed shell road and the kitchen building opposite.

The island mural on the opposite wall had been skillfully

painted by a local artist. Even though it was nothing more than a hallway, like everything else on the island it had been designed and decorated with care.

Alex rapped his knuckle on Harriet's door and walked in. She stood at her windows, a barefoot vision of loveliness in a pale green silk suit that skimmed her curves and set off her golden hair. He appreciated that the skirt stopped just shy of her nicely shaped knees.

She was bouncing a smooth round beach stone from hand to hand while she stared out the window. When she saw him she set the stone on her desk and hurried over to greet him.

"I've been waiting for you," she said, and stepped close enough to plant a kiss on his cheek.

Alex grabbed her around the waist and pulled her in for a real kiss. As he deepened the kiss and Harriet responded, all thoughts of murder flew from his mind. There was only Harriet, this lovely creature who loved him. He reluctantly broke off the kiss when he remembered where they were and why he was there.

"So." He leaned his forehead against hers, easy to do since she stood nearly six foot in bare feet.

"So," she repeated. Her voice sounded huskier than usual to her ears. Embarrassed, she took a step back and cleared her throat.

"Lemonade or water?" she asked brightly. "I could use something to drink."

She busied herself at her small refreshment bar while she willed her heart to stop racing. Alex awakened a fire in her that she hadn't known she possessed until the first time he had kissed her. It was mortifying to realize how little it took to make her want to tear off her clothes–and his–and throw herself on him.

So unladylike of her. Wanton. And it felt marvelous.

Harriet set both lemonades on the bamboo and glass coffee table and plopped down onto one of the cushioned rattan chairs. Other than the rosewood desk which had been a surprise addition from the resort's decorator, Jan, her office was light and airy with bamboo, rattan, and glass furnishings and the soft colors of peach and teal and pale beige.

Alex took a seat opposite Harriet and grinned at her. He knew how flustered she got when he kissed her. He liked it. In fact he was downright proud of the effect he had on Harriet Monroe.

Harriet saw Alex's wicked grin and thanked heaven she was sitting down. Alex's grins had a way of turning her knees to water. It really was unfair of him to affect her so easily.

"So," she said again. "About last night . . ."

"Which part of last night? I remember two very distinct parts. One far more pleasant than the other."

Harriet flushed. "I thought you were here to talk about Adrian Pelookie's murder."

Alex dropped the playful banter immediately. Harriet was right. He was there to investigate a murder, not flirt with the woman of his dreams.

"You're right, I am. I know we were together last night at the party but could you please walk me through what you remember?"

Harriet relayed the events leading up to the moment they left Adrian standing at the table.

"Adrian was angry," she recalled.

Alex gave her a sharp look. "What do you mean, angry? What makes you say that?"

"Remember when she whipped the silk cloth away from the busts? She was watching the crowd with a look of-of . . . anticipation, I guess you could say. She was expecting a certain reaction, and when she didn't get it she looked at the ice sculptures and grew angry."

Alex mulled over Harriet's observations. "Adrian was expecting a reaction because she was responsible for the scarlet A. She didn't know that Chef Fritola had colored all of the sculptures so the A no longer stood out."

Harriet nodded. "That's what I think. I don't think that means that Adrian was responsible for Arlo's death, though. Why would she kill him?"

"To cover up the fact that she was responsible for the scarlet A?"

"No." Harriet tucked her long legs beneath her and took a minute to put her thoughts in order.

"Adrian wanted a reaction from a specific someone. Maybe more than one someones. She wouldn't care if they knew she had put the A on her mother's bust. Adrian might even have wanted everyone to know that she was responsible for the A. If that's true then she had no reason to kill Arlo because she had nothing to cover up."

Alex sipped his lemonade, enjoying the sweet tart flavor after drinking too many cups of coffee that morning.

"Okay," he said slowly. 'I think you might be onto something. Who was she trying to shock with the A?"

"I think we can assume that the A did not stand for Adelaide. I keep thinking about the story Bennet told me about the adulteress who had to wear a scarlet A on her dress so everyone would know she was a sinner and therefore they should ostracize her. What if the A harkens back to that?"

"You think Adrian's mother is an adulteress."

"Or was." Harriet lifted a hand, let it drop to her lap. "I don't know, but it's a place to start."

Alex waggled his head from to side. "Okay, let's assume that Adelaide is unfaithful to her husband and Adrian finds out somehow. Why would she stage a public spectacle? Wouldn't she be embarrassing herself as well as her mother?"

"Maybe she wanted to shame her mother." Harriet

warmed to the idea. '*Maybe* Adrian wanted to move up in the Pelookie organization and Adelaide stood in her way. It wouldn't be the first time a child ousted a parent and took their place in the family business. Maybe the A was Adrian firing a shot across Adelaide's bow."

"It's possible, I guess, but I'm not sold. Fox and I spoke to Adrian's father this morning. Apparently Adrian was a serial dater. Bennet did not approve of her free and easy lifestyle at all."

Harriet's eyes lit up. She leaned forward, excited. "Don't you see? Like mother, like daughter. Adelaide sleeps around, Adrian sleeps around."

"Again, possible," Alex agreed, "but it still doesn't feel right. Remember, there was no reaction from the Pelookie clan when Adrian unveiled the ice sculptures. It turned out to be no big deal. Did you happen to notice who she was looking at when she pulled the cloth off the busts?"

Harriet shook her head. "No. The three brothers and Adelaide were standing together directly in front of Adrian. Samuel and Richard had women with them. Their wives, I assume. It was impossible to tell which one Adrian was looking at, at least from where we were standing. And she didn't get a reaction because the A was no longer visible. I think that's important."

Alex set his empty lemonade glass on the table and stood.

"Thanks for your input. It helps."

A warm glow filled Harriet. Alex had thanked her for her input. He valued her. It pleased her that Alex seriously considered her thoughts and opinions and trusted her enough to discuss Adrian and Arlo's murder with her.

Alex was so different from her ex. Bradley had treated her like she was an airhead until she had begun to believe it herself.

Harriet stood to walk Alex to the door. He stared down at

her with those impossibly blue eyes. The smoldering heat in them made something in her belly flutter. She forgot to breathe for a long minute. Would he kiss her again? She fervently hoped so. She loved his kisses.

Alex's slow smile told her that he knew what was going through her mind. To her intense disappointment, instead of closing the distance between them, he took a step back.

"I have to go start my other interviews and check in with Fox. I'll share your theories with him. Thanks for the lemonade. And for the coffee this morning. It was a wonderful surprise."

Harriet struggled to hide her disappointment. She really needed to get a grip on herself where Alex was concerned but the man frustrated her. Why was he holding back on moving their relationship forward?

She was ready for more. She knew Alex loved her. He didn't try to hide it. It was a truly sad thing that at her age she knew next to nothing about how a proper romance should progress. She stifled a sigh and reminded herself to be patient.

"Will I see you later?" she asked, in as nonchalant a manner as she could muster while they walked to the door together.

Alex leaned down and set a chaste kiss on Harriet's soft cheek. Then he couldn't help himself. He dropped another kiss on the sensitive spot below her ear and grinned when she shivered and caught her breath.

Harriet felt his smile against her skin. She pressed her arms to her sides to keep from wrapping them around Alex's neck. She wanted to snuggle her body as close to his as she could get. She would pull off his shirt and . . . her face flushed when the image of a magnificent, naked Alex filled her brain.

Again.

Apparently Alex had awakened a hot and steamy side of her personality that she hadn't known she possessed.

"Come by anytime you can't sleep," Alex whispered in her ear before letting himself out.

Harriet couldn't stop the shiver his warm breath induced. She heard Alex's soft chuckle as she closed the door behind him. The wretched man. He knew exactly how he affected her.

CHAPTER FOURTEEN

Harriet decided she needed to get out of her office after Alex's visit. She didn't have the experience to know how to get what she wanted from him so once again he had left her feeling flustered and not a little frustrated, both conditions that made it hard for her to concentrate on either paperwork or editing footage for her next advertisement for the resort.

The first group of underprivileged kids were scheduled to arrive on the island at the end of the week. She decided to go check with the resort attractions most likely to appeal to the children and make triple sure everything was ready for them.

Satisfied that she had a legitimate reason to leave her office, Harriet left her heels under her desk, put on her trainers, and checked in with Cassie to see if the resort director needed anything from her before Harriet commandeered a resort cart and headed to the marina.

The marina was a popular attraction for all the resort guests, adult and child alike. Harriet felt sure the underprivileged children would be no exception.

Set on the resort's west shore nearly two-thirds of the way up the coastline from the island's southern tip, the marina possessed every water toy ever invented. At least it seemed that way to Harriet.

Water toys were not a common sight on the cold North Atlantic off the coast of Maine where she grew up. Even in the hottest part of summer only the most hardy of souls were able to spend much time in the frigid ocean water. Most waded in up to their knees, took a quick dip and ran back out, shrieking about the cold.

The mental image made Harriet smile. It was hard to believe the cold North Atlantic water and the warm, turquoise waters surrounding the Island Resort were part of the same ocean.

They were as different as . . . well, as different as her life in Maine had been compared to her life on the resort. Night and day. Sucky and fabulous.

Harriet pulled into the marina's crushed shell parking lot and parked outside the main office. She found Leonard Dixon, the marina's manager, inside the office handing out sunscreen to a mother with two adolescent boys.

The excited boys whooped and hollered their way past Harriet when she entered the office. Harriet had to grin when their mother shouted at the boys to wait, rolled her eyes at Harriet, and threw out an apology before running after the excited youngsters.

Harriet turned her grin on the man behind the counter. "Good morning, Leonard. I thought I'd check on preparations for my kids since they'll be arriving in a few days."

The marina office was light and airy with large windows on two right-angled walls overlooking the parking area and the docks.

Pale teal walls trimmed in white gave the space a beachy look. A waist high counter jutted from the right hand wall into the center of the room. Behind it stood two steel-blue metal desks, only one of which was being used.

After unexpectedly losing his second-in-command, Leonard had yet to fill the position of assistant manager.

"Hey, Harry. I was wondering if you'd stop by." Leonard put away the sunscreen options the mother had not wanted and smiled at Harriet.

An average sized man, Leonard stood a couple inches shorter than Harriet. With his average height and average looks, Leonard could easily be overlooked if it wasn't for his killer whiskey-colored eyes framed in thick, black lashes.

Those warm brown eyes looked bloodshot and tired.

"Baby not sleeping well?" Harriet asked sympathetically.

Leonard covered a yawn and blinked. "Sorry. No one's sleeping well. Baby Rose is teething. Judging from the amount of drool that runs from her mouth and her constant fussing, it's a bitch. Poor little tyke is miserable so naturally Dorinda and I are both miserable for her."

"I know you wouldn't trade a moment of it so don't think you're getting any sympathy from me."

They grinned at each other. Harriet liked Leonard Dixon and his wife Dorinda. They were an easy-going, down to earth couple who normally took whatever life tossed at them in stride. Leonard also had the patience of a saint, a trait that came in handy when dealing with the variety of personalities that used the marina.

"We're ready for your kids, Harry," Leonard assured her. "Not to worry. My crew is looking forward to showing them a good time. It's a wonderful program that you came up with and everyone here is excited to be a part of it."

Leonard's words warmed Harriet's heart. Since coming up with the idea of bringing groups of corporate sponsored children for a week's stay at the resort she'd heard nothing but positive feedback and offers of help. The resort had an exceptional group of generous and kind employees.

"I've activated extra droids so we can teach them how to

use the kayaks one on one," Leonard continued. "We'll also have fishing rods for anyone who wants to try their hand at fishing. I think we'll get a few takers. And we'll have one boat prepped to take anyone who doesn't want to fish off the docks offshore to fish. I've had several hotel employees volunteer their free time to help out so we can keep an eye on everyone."

A teenaged boy entered the office to sign out a personal water jet. Leonard recited the rules, secured a life vest on him, cautioned him to stay in sight of the island and finally told him to have fun. The kid left with a big grin on his face.

"What about giving them a ride on the glass bottomed boats?" Harriet asked. "I think the children would be fascinated to see the coral reefs and all the beautiful fish that live around the island."

Leonard nodded. "That's a great idea, Harry. I'll schedule both glass bottomed boats so we can take the whole group out at the same time." He made a note on his personal pc.

"Several of the droids are programmed to teach any of the kids who'd like to learn how to swim, but they probably won't have enough time to get confident enough to snorkel. Seeing what's under the surface from the boats will come close."

Harriet shook her head in amazement. "It all sounds wonderful, Leonard. Thank you for going above and beyond. I have a feeling the marina will be very popular with the children."

"I hope so. I'm looking forward to meeting them all. Dorinda wants to help out too. She and Rose are going to come by for a few hours every afternoon to cover the office so I can be on the docks."

"Great! I'll have to swing by so I can see how much Rose has grown. If you don't mind I thought I'd wander the docks for a bit this morning before I head back to my office–just in case anything else occurs to me."

After Leonard waved her off Harriet made her way to the four large main docks. Power and sailboats of every size filled the small finger docks that jutted off each large dock like limbs of a stylized drawing of a tree.

Two docks housed sailboats ranging in size from small one person sailing dinghies to large overnight cruisers for any guests who wanted to explore the nearby islands. The sailboats rocked gently in the waves, their metal rigging clanging gently against the masts.

Besides the clear-bottomed boats which were very popular with the resort guests, the marina also had boats for sightseeing, fishing, waterskiing, and parasailing. There were even three pontoon boats for partying in the quiet waters of the island's west side coves.

All of the smallest boats and sailboards were painted florescent orange to make them easier to spot if a guest became lost or got into trouble. The ski-jets and larger boats had tracking devices built into them and could be tracked individually. A droid captain was required on all the overnight cruisers.

So far the resort hadn't lost a single guest.

Other than the ones who had been murdered, that was.

Harriet shook off the thought. She stood at the far end of the nearest dock and looked down into the clear water. Small waves slapped at nearby hulls and against the dock's weathered gray boards. The air smelled of water and seaweed, brine and green vegetation.

She took several deep breaths and released them on a happy sigh. She could never live away from the ocean. Warm or frigid, it was all she knew.

Green fronds of seaweed had attached themselves to the

dock's wooden pilings. They swayed to and fro with the water's movements, like ribbons twisting in the wind.

Giant red starfish and blue-black mussels clung to any piling spots left bare by the seaweed. A spiny sea urchin moved slowly across the bottom, its stiff, pale green spines waving as it searched for food.

Sun rays glinted off the sea beyond the marina and fractured into thousands of points of light. The beauty of it all was almost too much to bear. Harriet hadn't spent much time at the marina since coming to work on the island because she'd been too busy. It was time to change that.

The marina reminded her of Portland's working waterfront. When she and Solly were young runaways they had spent many hours scrounging the docks for food and watching the fishing boats—usually chased by flocks of raucous white gulls—come and go.

The resort's marina didn't smell of tar and rotting baitfish like the Portland waterfront had, but it had the same busy atmosphere.

Harriet was deep in thought, thinking up an ad angle to showcase the marina's offerings while she headed back to her cart, when a woman jumped off a boat's aft deck and collided with her, nearly sending both of them tumbling over the side of the dock.

Harriet instinctively grabbed the woman's arm so she wouldn't lose her balance and fall back onto the boat.

There was something familiar about the woman. Curvy and petite with a mass of red curls a little redder than nature ever provided, it took Harriet a few moments to place her.

"Mrs. Pelookie? You're Samuel's wife, aren't you? I saw you at the party last night with your husband. Are you all right? I should have been paying closer attention. I'm so sorry I ran into you."

CHAPTER FIFTEEN

Mrs. Pelookie's eyes had the slightly unfocused look of someone who'd been drinking a bit too much. Even though she had run into Harriet, Harriet knew better than to accuse her.

"I'm fine." Mrs. Pelookie swayed slightly. "I'm fine," she repeated more firmly, trying to dislodge Harriet's hand from her arm.

Harriet didn't think the woman looked fine. She couldn't just leave her there. What if Mrs. Pelookie fell off the dock and drowned before anyone noticed? The resort did not need another death.

"I'm Harriet Monroe. Public Relations Director for the resort. Can I give you a lift back to the hotel? I was just heading that way."

Big green eyes blinked up at her. Mrs. Pelookie had the petite build that often made Harriet feel like a giant ogress.

Harriet had to repeat her question. She kept a firm hold on the swaying Mrs. Pelookie.

"All right." Mrs. Pelookie finally nodded, then shook her head. "But I'm staying in a cottage, not the hotel." She spoke slowly, taking care to enunciate her words, a common technique used by drunks who think they can hide the extent of their drunkenness.

"No problem, Mrs. Pelookie. I'm driving right by the coves. Which one are you in?" Harriet placed her hand under the woman's elbow to steady her as she led her off the dock.

"Call me Val. My name is Valerie, but everyone calls me Val. I hate being called Mrs. Pelookie. Adelaide is Mrs. Pelookie. We're staying in Black Bart's Cove. *Black Bart.* What a name to be stuck with. He was a pirate you know."

Val peered at Harriet through fake lashes long enough to sweep the floor with. Harriet couldn't take her eyes off those outrageous eyelashes. Why did women feel the need to do that to themselves? Especially older women, like she knew Valerie must be. They ended up looking like clowns more often than not. Although she had to admit that Valerie Pelookie looked great, even with the fake lashes.

Then again, what did she know? She was crazy in love with a man who apparently had no trouble keeping his hands off her despite the fact that she practically threw herself at him. Maybe she should try fluttering some false eyelashes at Alex.

Val misinterpreted Harriet's sudden grin. "Black Bart. Black black Bart. A pirate with a black black heart." She chuckled at her own cleverness. "Do you know the cove with the sunken pirate's ship?"

"I'm familiar with it, yes." The west side of the island had several beautiful coves, four of which had cottages for guests who preferred not to stay in the hotel. Her friend Payson lived in the end cottage on Kidd's Cove. Black Bart's Cove with its partially sunken ship was popular with families who had older kids who liked to snorkel or dive the wreck.

"We'll just grab this cart right here and be on our way."

Harriet kept her hand under Valerie's elbow until she had settled her into the cart.

Valerie gripped the dashboard and the top of the door when Harriet started the cart. Harriet suppressed a smile. Did Valerie think Harriet was going to speed away in the cart? Impossible, as the hydrogen powered carts had a top speed of thirty miles an hour.

"I'm sorry about your niece," Harriet said after driving for several minutes in silence.

Valerie snorted. "Good riddance is all I have to say." She drummed her fingers on the cart's dashboard. "Although I do feel sorry for Bennet. He adored his daughter."

Harriet wasn't sure how to respond to Valerie's lack of sympathy for the dead woman. And why didn't Valerie feel any sympathy for Adrian's mother Adelaide?

"Good riddance?" Harriet repeated. "Did Adrian cause problems in the family?" she asked carefully.

Valerie rolled her eyes. "When *didn't* Adrian cause problems? That girl loved drama. Always did. She was always trying to stir things up between the brothers. I wouldn't be surprised to hear that she had arranged to have herself killed. I told Sammy we should skip Adrian's big *"event"*–she put finger quotes around the word event–"but he was afraid we'd miss something. Turns out he was right." She cackled and snorted again.

Harriet frowned at her passenger. "Don't the brothers get along? From what Adrian had told me I got the impression that the Pelookies are a close knit family."

Valerie shrugged. "Oh, the brothers are close all right. Maybe a little too close." She shrugged one shoulder and turned her head to watch the jungle.

Harriet waited for several minutes hoping that Valerie would say more, but Valerie seemed more interested in the lizards darting along the side of the road than saying anything further.

Harriet wanted to hear more about the Pelookie family. Maybe she'd learn something that would help Alex find the murderer. She tried to think of a way to get Val talking again.

"I never had close family. It must be nice," Harriet prodded, "to be surrounded by people who love you–"

Valerie's head whipped around to look at Harriet. "Close family isn't nice when you have a sister-in-law that all the brothers constantly fawn over. It's sickening, is what it is. The rest of us get tired of always playing second fiddle."

"They 'fawn' over your sister-in-law? In what way?" Harriet decreased the cart's speed slightly and hoped Valerie wouldn't notice. She needn't have worried. Valerie had warmed to what was obviously a favorite complaint.

"Sammy and Richie and Bennie suck up to Queen Adelaide, that's what I mean. I'm sick of it. Sick of it," Valerie muttered. She waved one hand in the air. "It's like she's some-some sort of . . . *goddess* or something. I'll admit that she's beautiful. What man wouldn't notice. But the way those men act around her is beyond the pale."

"They *are* in business together," Harriet pointed out. "Maybe they're simply good friends."

Valerie snorted and shot Harriet an unbelieving look. "Don't be stupid. She might act like she's upper class, but Adelaide Pelookie is nothing but a common whore who married well. Whoever put that scarlet A on her ice sculpture had the right of it. Too bad your chef found a way to disguise it. I'd like to have seen her face when Adrian whipped off the cloth."

Unfortunately for Harriet they had reached the narrow lane marked with a pale gray plinth with "Black Bart's Cove" carved vertically into the stone.

"We're in the third cottage," Valerie told her when they reached the cove.

"Right." Harriet tried to come up with a last question before the opportunity for inside information on the family disappeared. As she pulled onto the parking pad next to Valerie's cottage she thought of something.

"Why did you say that Adelaide is a whore?" she asked while Valerie climbed out of the cart. "That's a pretty serious allegation.

Valerie slammed the cart door and leaned over it. She glared at Harriet.

"*Because.*" Valerie leaned into the cart so far Harriet wondered if she was going to fall back in. Her green eyes snapped with anger and her lips curled into a contemptuous sneer.

"*Because,*" she repeated, "the bitch slept with my husband."

She turned and stormed off, leaving Harriet with her jaw hanging open.

CHAPTER SIXTEEN

Although Alex and Fox thoroughly searched the area where Alex had found Adrian's body, they found no clues to help them. The soft sand held no footprints. The coconut husk with its covering of fine hairs held no fingerprints, only blood from Adrian's head wound.

The killer hadn't dropped a conveniently monogrammed personal item and if they had lost a hair or two the ocean breeze had carried it off the previous night.

Based on his conviction that Arlo and Adrian's murders were connected, Alex sent Fox to re-interview the kitchen staff. Solve one murder and they would solve them both. He also put in a call to Dr. Clarke but the doctor had no new information for him.

Adrian Pelookie had died from several blows to the head with a coconut.

Arlo Caminiti had frozen to death.

Tox screens on both came back clean. Adrian had an empty stomach and a negligible blood alcohol level. Arlo had eaten a meal of pasta with red sauce approximately three hours before his death. Both victims were otherwise healthy and should have lived long lives.

Alex set the murders aside and hopped on his black, vintage Triumph Tiger. He had rebuilt the bike in his NYC apartment, a labor of love that had taken him nearly three years and helped him hang onto his sanity when he found himself buried to his eyeballs in murders.

Despite the bike Alex had eventually grown soul sick from wading through death day in and day out. When he caught himself wondering if there was any point to life he realized that he needed to make a change and he needed to make it quick.

Douglas Wade's job offer couldn't have come at a better time.

Alex's only request before he signed on as the resort's security director was that he be able to bring the Tiger to the island with him.

Wade had balked at first. Gas powered combustion vehicles weren't allowed on the island. The resort carts, the four Road Hogs, and even the marina's power boats were all hydrogen powered. No pollution, no noise to interfere with the island's serenity.

When Alex held firm about bringing the motorbike or not taking the position, Wade caved and agreed to let Alex bring the Triumph with him.

Because the bike was loud compared to the silent resort carts and Alex didn't want to abuse the privilege, he limited his use of the bike. He used it when his destination was too far to walk and limited his joy rides to the less inhabited parts of the island.

He found riding the bike especially useful when he needed to sort his thoughts. Puzzle pieces–and what else was murder but a type of puzzle–often fell into place when he allowed his thoughts to drift.

He also used the bike when he was short of time and needed to get somewhere fast. The resort carts were comfortable and attractive with their turquoise blue paint and chrome finishes, but they were often too damn slow to suit his needs.

Responding to Payson's summons when he was short of time justified using the Tiger. He fired it up and roared up the resort's main road, reveling in the bike's speed and power. Unfortunately the trip to Kidd's Cove was far too short.

Alex cut the bike's engine and drifted in silence the last twenty feet to Payson's cottage. Set apart from the regular guest cottages strung along the shallow, white sand beach that lined Kidd's Cove, Payson's cottage was never rented out to resort guests.

A close friend of Douglas Wade, Payson lived full time in the cottage and kept a general eye on the resort for Wade while conducting his own business from the cottage's second bedroom.

Alex had no clue what type of business Payson was in, but he had once caught a glimpse of the second bedroom's highly sophisticated tech set-up before Payson had closed the door.

Since Payson firmly protected his privacy Alex had never felt right questioning him about what he'd seen, but his already significant respect and admiration for Payson's intelligence and tech savvy had risen several more notches that day.

Alex parked the Tiger and rounded the side of the cottage. He found Payson on his lanai deadheading a flowering shrub. Payson was dressed casually, in loose, white cotton pants, bare feet, and a flowing, natural linen tunic that accentuated his slim build. His thick white hair was brushed straight back from his face and tied in a short queue.

Payson reminded Alex of a guru who had taken the US by

storm a decade earlier. Mahatma Jo? He couldn't remember. Gurus all seemed to possess variations of the same name.

Alex bounded up the three steps to the lanai while he tried to get a read on Payson's mood. It was unusual for him to be summoned to the cottage without being told why beforehand.

He took a deep breath of the heady fragrance from the flowers. He had no idea what they were, but the scent reminded him of spice and sweet jasmine and Harriet.

These days it seemed that everything made him think of Harriet.

"You wanted to see me, Payson?"

Payson gave Alex a warm smile. "Yes. Thank you for accommodating me, Alex. I wanted to discuss something with you and I didn't feel like dressing for a trip to your office. Come inside and I'll get you a beer unless you'd prefer something else."

That was another thing about the older man that Alex had noticed. Payson always managed to look elegant and put together whenever he left his cottage. It was unusual to see Payson dressed in relaxed clothing, yet somehow he still managed to look elegant.

Alex guessed that Payson could look elegant dressed in rags. There was just something about the man that oozed grace and style. The elegance was an essential characteristic that was part of Payson, Alex realized. Clothes didn't make Payson look elegant, Payson made anything he wore look elegant.

He wondered what it meant that Payson hadn't dressed up for his visit. Maybe nothing. Maybe something. Maybe Payson didn't feel the need to impress Alex. Or maybe he considered Alex a friend. Alex hoped so. He had a great liking for the older man and would feel honored to count him as a friend.

"A beer would taste wonderful." Alex told him as he followed Payson inside the cottage.

The cottage was not the largest on Kidd's Cove, having only two bedrooms, but it was more spacious than the resort's other two bedroom guest cottages.

Alex suspected that Wade had constructed the cottage to Payson's specifications. It had several features that the other cottages did not possess, such as a state of the art security system and one-way shields on the windows.

He took a seat in a comfortably worn leather chair in the living room and stretched his long legs out in front of him while Payson glided off to the kitchen for refreshments.

The living room walls were covered with an impressive collection of carved wooden masks of every size and facial expression. Alex knew from previous visits that most of the masks were centuries old and all were quite valuable.

He inspected a mask on the opposite wall carved from a highly figured, golden wood. The face looked soft and feminine, with high cheek bones, large eyes, and generous lips. What was its story? Did the carver use a model? If so it must have been someone the artist cared for, given the beauty of the mask.

"Here you are. I hope you like India Pale Ale. It's all I have in the fridge at the moment." Payson set a coaster on the coffee table next to Alex and placed the beer on it before settling into another equally worn leather chair.

"We aren't any closer to solving the two murders if that's what you wanted to speak with me about," Alex told him. He took a long swallow of the cold beer, appreciating the hoppy, citrusy flavor. "I know the murders are related but I can't see how yet."

Payson listened intently while Alex laid out what he knew about the deaths of Arlo and Adrian.

"So Arlo was in a good frame of mind the last time anyone spoke with him," Payson verified.

Alex nodded. "Yep. One person even called him giddy. Said he hinted at good things happening."

"Given Arlo's status in life up until the day he died, I daresay that in Arlo's mind, a good thing happening was most likely money related."

Alex pursed his lips. "So you're suggesting that someone paid Arlo for access to the freezer and then killed Arlo so he couldt' identify whoever it was?"

Payson shrugged. "Makes sense to me."

Alex took a deep breath and let it out followed by a long pull on his beer.

"Makes sense to me too. The only reason I can see for a non-kitchen staff member to want to get inside the freezer would be to paint the scarlet A on Adelaide Pelookie's bust."

"I agree."

"So these murders are related to the scarlet A, which means that the Pelookie family is at the heart of this." Alex looked at Payson expectantly. "Do you have any background on Adelaide?"

The question wasn't out of the blue. In the past Payson had proved to be a valuable source of inside information. An image of the high tech equipment in the other room popped into Alex's mind. Just what did Payson use it for?

Payson's pale blue eyes twinkled at the question. "Adelaide Sawyer was considered a real beauty three decades ago. No one had heard of her until she popped up on the public radar about a year before she married Bennet Pelookie."

"Do you have any background on her during that year before she married Bennet?"

A faint blush colored Payson's cheeks. "Adelaide was very . . . popular . . . before her marriage, you could say. I knew of her although we were never introduced. She liked to party back then as I recall, and because of her beauty she was often seen on the arm of wealthy men at charity functions. I suspect that's how she met Bennet."

Payson shook his head. "As far as Adelaide's earlier life, no, I don't know anything."

Alex nodded. "Okay, I'll dig around more, see what I turn up. Thanks, Payson." He sipped his beer and waited. Something told him that the murders were not the reason Payson had asked him to come by the cottage. Payson didn't keep him waiting long.

"I wanted to speak with you about Harriet, Alex," he said slowly. "I've lined up a good specialist to help her but I think it would be unfair to drop this on her without trying to prepare her beforehand."

"I agree." Unable to sit still while talking about a subject that angered him to his core, Alex sprang up and began to pace Payson's living room.

"I don't want getting her to see a specialist to be underhanded," Alex stopped pacing and faced Payson. "The problem is that every time she thinks about her parents and what happened she gets a terrible headache. I tried asking her what she remembers about her early years and the sudden pain she suffered was excruciating."

Alex thought back to the night he had tried to get Harriet to open up about her past.

"I didn't know then what her aunt had done to her and I made the mistake of pushing Harriet to remember. The physical pain got so bad that she passed out cold. When she came to again she didn't remember anything about our conversation. That quack doctor her aunt hired put some obscenely powerful mental blocks in Harriet's head. The poor girl gets a headache as soon as she thinks about anything to do with her parents."

"We have to prepare her before she sees the specialist,"

Payson insisted. "We won't push her to remember, but I think we need to tell her that her aunt had her memories blocked and why we want her to see the specialist. Harriet is a very intelligent woman, Alex. She won't fight this if she understands that we're trying to help her."

Alex looked out at the shining cove and ran a hand through his hair. The memory of the pain Harriet had suffered that night still haunted him.

"I can't bear to see her in that kind of pain again, Payson," he said softly.

"I understand, son. Consider this. Harriet is an adult now. She didn't have a choice when the mental blocks were put in. Her aunt took that choice away from her. She deserves to have a choice now. We need to tell her as much as she can handle. If the pain becomes too much for her to bear we can back off. But we have to try. And I think we should do it together."

Alex continued to stare out at the cove for several long minutes. He knew that if he and Harriet were going to have a fair shot at a happy marriage and a family that she needed to deal with her past.

Finally he turned and nodded at Payson. "You're right, of course. I can't just take her to a head doctor without any explanation."

He returned to his chair and leaned toward Payson with his elbows on his knees and his hands dangling. "When do you want to talk to her? I agree that it would be best if we did it together. She's very fond of you and she trusts you–you've become like a favorite uncle to her."

Payson looked pleased. "I am also very fond of her. If I had a daughter I would want her to be like Harriet. The girl has a big heart and a keen intellect and a sweet disposition."

He picked up a personal PC from the table next to his chair and checked its calendar.

"Harriet's first group of underprivileged children arrives in two days. She'll be completely focused on them while they're here. Let's wait to talk with her until they leave. I don't want anything to spoil her enjoyment of the children's visit."

Alex took a deep breath and let it out. "Okay. We'll tell Harriet about what her aunt did to her and how we propose to fix it the day after the children leave."

He stood and headed to the door. "I pray we can help her," he said over his shoulder on his way out. A moment later the Triumph roared to life and left.

"I hope we can help her too, son," Payson replied quietly to the empty cottage.

He was exceedingly fond of Harriet Monroe. Unbeknownst to Alex, Payson had been aware of Harriet's horrific history well before her arrival on the island.

He had kept track of the young girl ever since the horrendous day her parents and seventy other men, women, and children had followed their insane leader and ended their lives with an overdose of an illegal street drug known then as Blitz.

Only Harriet had survived.

After the mass suicide Payson had vowed that he would do everything in his power to help the lone survivor. It was the only thing he could think of to help ease his pain over the loss of his younger sister that same day.

And if he was going to be brutally honest with himself, he hoped that once Harriet regained her memories of her time with the cult, she would be able to tell him about his sister's last days.

CHAPTER SEVENTEEN

Harriet checked Alex's office after she dropped Valerie off at Black Bart's Cove, but he wasn't around. She could have tagged him on his link but she knew he was busy hunting down a killer and if he was interviewing someone or catching up on sleep she didn't want to interrupt him.

She headed home, took a shower, and crawled into her bed even though the sun had yet to set. Lack of sleep the previous night coupled with a busy day had worn her out and she slept the night through without dreaming.

By the time she awoke the following morning the sun's rays slanted across the water in front of Mermaid Cottage with a soft, buttery light and the seagulls were calling. She sent a quick text to Alex telling him she needed to see him when he had a spare minute and crawled out of bed.

A quick shower, toasted bagel with fresh pineapple juice, and Harriet was on her way to her office. Drops of dew still coated the leaves of plants that grew low to the ground, sparkling like hidden pearls and revealing intricate spider webs that she wouldn't have noticed otherwise.

She loved the morning walk to work. Every day it seemed

that she discovered something new on the island. She stopped to watch a small chameleon that waited for prey to come along, unseen because it blended with the flowered shrub it sat on, its body camouflaged in brilliant green and red.

How did the little lizard know what color to be? It seemed like pure magic.

A flurry of red wings exploded from the trees high overhead with a great deal of chatter before settling into another nearby group of trees. Red macaws, according to Solly.

She would have liked to stop and watch the colorful parrots but she needed to get to her office and call Alex. She needed to tell him about her conversation with Valerie Pelookie.

Her heart fluttered when she found him waiting for her in the lobby, his broad shoulders propped against a wall as he worked his personal pc.

He looked up when she entered and smiled at her, revealing the dimple in his right cheek.

The small flutter in Harriet's heart spread through her entire body.

"Good morning, Alex. Good morning, Jeeves." She was proud of how cool and professional her voice sounded. The droid greeted her and moved to the locked hall door to let her in.

"You wanted to see me?" Alex pushed himself off the wall and put away his pocket computer.

"Yes. Let's talk in my office."

Harriet led the way down the hall without speaking and stopped to engage her palm plate. She tried to ignore the heat coming off Alex's body as he stood directly behind her, but good lord, it was difficult. Every cell in her body yearned to cuddle closer to that heat.

As soon as they entered the office Harriet moved to stand

behind her desk to put some space between them, ignoring her body's protest at the loss of his nearness.

"What are you shaking your head at?"

Embarrassed, Harriet dropped her backpack on the desk. "I was shaking my head?" Because she couldn't come up with a plausible reason other than the truth–that she wanted him with every fiber in her body–she said nothing.

"Yes." Alex moved to the opposite side of the desk and inspected her. "You look rested this morning."

Relieved to have a safe topic to discuss, Harriet nodded. "I went to bed early and slept through the night. How about you? Did you get much sleep?"

She noted the fine lines at the outer corners of Alex's tired eyes and answered her own question.

"You were up late again, weren't you?"

"Yes. I had background research on the Pelookie's to do. What did you want to tell me?"

Suddenly aware that she was taking up his valuable time, Harriet mentally kicked herself and hurried on with what she had to say.

"I met Valerie Pelookie yesterday at the marina. She was pretty unsteady on her feet–it was fairly obvious that she'd been drinking. I gave her a lift back to the cottage she and Samuel are staying in and she said something that I thought you should hear."

She told him about Valerie's opinion of Adelaide Pelookie and her parting shot about Adelaide sleeping with Valerie's husband.

She appreciated the way Alex listened without interruption until she had finished. He was good that way, a trait she knew must have helped him when he'd been a NYC murder detective.

He frowned when she finished and drummed the fingers of one hand on her desktop.

"Interesting. I dug into Adelaide last night. Adelaide Sawyer was definitely a party girl before she married Bennet Pelookie. Reading between the lines I'd say she was rather loose with her sexual favors with a penchant for wealthy men. Valerie didn't say if this encounter between Adelaide and Samuel happened before or after Valerie married him?"

Harriet shook her head. "No. I assumed Valerie was telling me that it happened after they were married, but it could have been before I guess."

Alex began to wander the room. He always thought better when he was on the move. He put his hands in his pockets and wandered to the large glass lanai doors. A lone jogger moved slowly just above the waves lapping the beach. Sunlight gleamed off a dolphin as it carved an arc back into the water beyond the jogger.

Another day in paradise. If it wasn't for two dead people he would be digging it.

Aware that Harriet was watching him, he stepped away from the window and moved to the wall of shelves where she kept the holo of her parents. He admired it without picking it up.

"You look like both your parents," he said, as he inspected the smiling, happy couple. They looked like any ordinary couple in love. Why would two intelligent, happy people commit suicide? It made no sense to him.

"Except for the bump on your nose." He turned toward Harriet with a smile. "When did that happen?"

She rubbed the bump on the bridge of her nose and frowned. "You know, I honestly have no idea. I don't remember breaking it although obviously I did. I asked my aunt about it once but she couldn't–or wouldn't–tell me what happened."

A dull ache began to throb at the back of Harriet's skull. Great. Another headache. She sat in her chair and found the pain blockers she kept in her top desk drawer, swallowing one dry.

Alex grabbed a tube of water from her fridge, cracked it, and handed it to her. "You shouldn't swallow those dry. Headache?"

Embarrassed by her weakness, Harriet took the water and drank it down. "Thanks. They pop up at the most inconvenient times. Fortunately they don't stick around long. I've read of migraine sufferers who are laid low for days, unable to function, until the headache passes."

Alex didn't pursue the subject. Given that Harriet had experienced a headache when talking about the broken nose he knew that it had to have occurred during those eight years that were blocked from her memory.

He fought the urge to take her in his arms and tell her that he knew the truth about her past. He wanted to tell her that he and Payson knew the reason behind the headaches and intended to help her recover her memories. But now wasn't the time or place so he kept his arms pressed to his sides and changed the subject.

"Okay, back to the Pelookie family." He leaned one hip against the side of her desk and looked down at her. "Valerie verifies that Adelaide's actions probably deserved a scarlet A. But–" he paused. "And this is a *big* but–I can't see that Valerie had any reason to kill Arlo and Adrian."

"Unless she found out about the scarlet A and thought people might find out that Adelaide had slept with her husband," Harriet pointed out.

"I don't think so. The motive is too weak. I think we can safely move Valerie to the bottom of the suspect list."

Harriet leaned back in her chair and looked up at Alex. The blocker had wiped out the headache making it easier to focus.

"It sounds as if you've narrowed your suspect list down to the Pelookie family. Have you?"

"I can't come up with a motive that explains both murders unless it's connected to the Pelookies. If Arlo's death was a personal thing then the killer had no reason to want Adrian dead too." He shook his head and pushed away from her desk.

"My gut tells me that one of the elder Pelookies is to blame. Hopefully I'll get to the bottom of this before they all leave Saturday."

"I have faith in you, Alex. You'll figure it out."

He leaned down and brushed Harriet's lips lightly with his own. He would have liked to lay a much more serious kiss on her but he didn't trust himself to stop with just a kiss.

"Speaking of Saturday," he said, straightening up and heading for the door, "what time do your kids arrive?"

Harriet's lips tingled. She bunched her fists to keep from touching them.

"The kids will be here mid-morning. The plan is to get them checked into their rooms and then give them a tour of the resort and lay out a few ground rules. Then I'm going to turn them loose." She smiled happily.

"You have a big heart, Harriet. What you're doing for these kids is wonderful."

A pensive look came over Harriet's face. "Solly and I were in the same boat as most of these kids, only we managed to avoid the orphanages and foster homes. Child Services means well but they're overwhelmed and understaffed and under financed.

"I know it isn't anywhere near enough, but if we can give these children one carefree week where they don't have to worry about personal safety or where they'll be sleeping, maybe it will show them that life has more to offer and give them something to work toward."

From tidbits that they dropped now and then Alex knew that Harriet and her friend Solly had had a tough time of it as homeless runaway teenagers. That they had matured into successful adults was attributed solely to their grit and hard work. No one had given either of them a helping hand.

"Like I said, what you're doing is wonderful."

Harriet shook off her sadness. Her eyes twinkled. "Wait until you see phase two of my plan."

Alex stopped at the door. "There's more?" he asked.

"Oh yeah. My next goal is to raise scholarship money to send every child who comes to the resort to uni or trade school—whichever suits them best. I don't want to simply tease them with a taste of what they can aspire to—I want to help them attain it."

"Harriet my love, you are a real jewel. My life is better for knowing you."

Alex's words warmed Harriet long after he left. She didn't know why he kept her at arm's length when he so obviously cared about her. Somehow she needed to find a way to let him know that she was ready for more.

CHAPTER EIGHTEEN

Richard Pelookie caught up with Harriet on her way to the employee's dining room for lunch. He grabbed her upper arm from behind and swung her around to face him.

"Bennet told me that you were with Hayes when he found Adrian's body," he accused.

No greeting. No polite, "May I have a moment of your time, Miss Monroe." Richard looked angry and his grip was painful, his fingers digging into her flesh.

Harriet pointedly stared at the hand holding her arm until Richard flushed and let her go. Once freed she took a step back to put herself out of the man's reach. Several employees walking by glanced her way. One young man stopped and stepped toward Harriet but she gave him a slight shake of her head and he continued on his way. The last thing she wanted was to be the focus of resort gossip. She would handle Richard on her own.

"Good day, Mr. Pelookie. Did you require something from me?" She put a little ice in her tone to let him know she wasn't happy with the way he'd grabbed her.

Richard ran his hand through his hair. It wasn't as dark as

his older brother Bennet's mane and contained no gray at all. Richard had the same large, beaked nose and dark brown eyes as the other brothers, but now that she looked at him more closely, Harriet was convinced that Richard had had some face and body work done.

"Is it true?" he demanded. "Did you see Adrian?"

"Yes." Harriet waited. What did the man want? She didn't feel comfortable discussing Adrian's murder with members of the Pelookie family and knew that Alex wouldn't want her to give the man any information.

"I was told someone hit her on the head. Did you know that?"

Harriet saw the pain in the man's eyes and felt a wave of sympathy.

"Yes, I knew that," she said gently. "I'm sorry for your loss, Mr. Pelookie."

"Richard, please." He smiled automatically, giving Harriet a glimpse of why women might find him attractive. She wondered suddenly if Richard Pelookie had also slept with Adelaide, either before or after her marriage to his older brother.

The thought made her squirm inside.

"Poor Adrian." Richard shook his head sadly. "She really tried, you know. She liked to party, it's true, but she wasn't just a party girl. Ree wanted to move up in the family business and take on more responsibility. She wanted to be groomed to take over Bennet's spot when he retired. Bennet told her that even though she was his daughter she had to climb the rungs like anyone else."

He sighed. "I'm afraid that didn't sit well with Adrian."

"Was Adrian capable of filling her father's shoes?"

Richard shrugged. "She was certainly smart enough. Ability was never an issue when it came to Adrian. She could do anything she set her mind too. But she had a tendency to go off the rails now and then."

Harriet frowned. "What does that mean? I don't understand. Are you saying Adrian acted out?"

"You could say that. She behaved herself and worked her butt off for months at a time but then–Kaboom! It was like she had to let off steam. She'd show up at the office dressed in party clothes from the night before and hung over from booze and whatever designer drug she'd taken."

"That must have been upsetting for her parents." Harriet checked her wrist unit. "You really should speak with our security director. Unless there is there something in particular you wanted from me, Mr. Pelookie?"

"I can't get any details out of Hayes. All he'll say is that Ree was hit on the head with a coconut. How can you kill a person with a coconut? I was hoping you could tell me more about how she died."

Harriet shook her head. "I'm sorry, I can't. Honestly? I don't know any more than that myself. Besides, any information really needs to come from Alex Hayes."

She saw the disappointment in Richard's eyes and relented a little. "I can tell you that the only wound I saw was on Adrian's head. That's all I know. I'm really sorry for your loss."

"Yeah. All right. I'm sorry I bothered you, Miss Monroe." Richard turned on his heel and walked off with his head down.

Harriet couldn't stop thinking about her conversation with Richard while she ate, and despite ordering one of her favorite meals she barely tasted her cajun fish tacos.

She finally gave up and left the dining room. Once outside she tagged Alex and asked him if she could swing by his office.

She found Alex five minutes later, waiting for her in the

security office lobby. His greeter droid Mary scanned Harriet briefly and returned to waiting mode behind the counter with her hands clasped behind her back and her feet spread apart, staring straight ahead.

Harriet followed Alex through the steel door that protected his wing of the building.

"Mary always looks so serious," she remarked while she waited for Alex to punch in the code that unlocked his office door. "She's a little intimidating–even a little creepy."

Alex shrugged. "She's not your friendly Jeeves droid, but I'd rather have Mary if I needed extra muscle."

Although constructed from the same pale stone as the other buildings in the resort, Harriet didn't particularly care for the security building. The lobby was pleasant enough with its gleaming wood floor, colorful padded chairs and green plants, but she found the rest of the building grim.

She considered Alex's office, located in a windowless wing that also housed a detention room for guests who needed to be locked up, and the island's only weapons locker, was the grimmest space of all.

Alex ushered Harriet into his office and closed the door behind her. He seemed distant, all business. Not the warm man who had complimented her on his way out of her office earlier that day. She had hoped for a kiss once they were alone but sensed that this was not the time. Alex was obviously in full murder cop mode.

"Have a seat." He slid behind his desk, a large, glossy black monstrosity that took up half the floor space in the small office. The desk's surface was clear except for an expensive comm system that she knew allowed him to connect with any other computer or communication system worldwide.

Harriet plopped down onto one of the black, hard metal chairs in front of Alex's desk and scanned the office. Nothing had changed since the last time she'd been in there. The wall next to the door held floor to ceiling shelves filled with forensic manuals and regulation and law books and not a single personal item.

That was it. The rest of the office walls were blank. No photos. No pictures. Not even a single window to let in natural light. Compared to her own light, airy office, Alex's had to be the most austere, grim work space she'd ever seen. She doubted that a monk's cell was even as austere as Alex's work space.

"So." Alex stretched out his legs and leaned back in his chair. He steepled his fingers and tapped them together, his favorite thinking mode. "What did you want to see me about?"

Harriet wasted no time telling Alex about the conversation she'd had with Richard.

"Adrian was moving up in the company," she concluded. "Maybe someone didn't like that and wanted her out of the way."

"Which would mean her murder had nothing to do with the scarlet A." Alex rubbed the space between his eyebrows. There were two many variables connected to the two murders and not enough evidence to follow.

"I'm sorry, Alex. I know this doesn't help, but I thought you should know."

He smiled at her then. "My inability to solve the murders is not your fault, Harriet. Unless you killed one of them?" He raised his scarred eyebrow in question.

"Ha-ha. Of course I didn't kill Arlo or Adrian. But have you considered that maybe you're looking for two killers, not one, like you originally thought?"

"Yeah, it's beginning to look that way. Unfortunately the Pelookie family leaves day after tomorrow. If I can't figure out who killed Adrian before then I'll have to either refuse to let them leave or turn everything I have over to the Miami detectives and let them deal with it when the Pelookies hit stateside."

Harriet knew by the tone of Alex's voice that he wasn't happy about the second possibility. While he had voluntarily made the choice to give up his career as a murder detective, Alex obviously had a competitive streak and felt the need to finish what he'd started.

She twisted her head around to watch him when he stood and paced the floor behind her seat. His brow furrowed and she knew he wasn't seeing his office any longer. His eyes had a faraway look in them.

"I made a classic rookie mistake assuming the two deaths are related." He stopped and frowned at Harriet. "Despite that fact I still can't shake the feeling that they're both connected to the scarlet A."

"Okay." Harriet thought for a minute. "What about this? If Arlo was responsible for painting the A on Adelaide's bust someone had to put him up to it. We already knew that. Right? He didn't think of painting that A all by himself."

Alex walked around the desk and slid back into his chair.

"Right. We can safely assume that someone in the Pelookie family hired Arlo to put that A on Adelaide's forehead. Why they did that, we don't yet know."

Harriet leaned forward. "If you hire someone to do something you generally pay them, either in cash or in favors. So what happened to the money, Alex? You searched Arlo's room and I assume you also checked his bank account?"

"Yes to both questions. There was no sign of any money beyond his regular salary deposits."

"Did whoever hired Arlo to paint the A kill him and take back the money? Maybe they were afraid Arlo would identify them?"

"Good question. But until we know why someone wanted the A painted on Adelaide's bust I don't think we can answer any of the other questions. Once we know why we'll know who."

"And we're back to the beginning," Harriet said. "How frustrating. Is this what most murder investigations are like?"

Alex gave her a half-smile. "Pretty much. You generally start with a lot of questions and eliminate suspects as you find the answers."

Harriet dug her personal pc out of her backpack. "Okay, first question: What does the scarlet A represent?" She looked at Alex and when he nodded she keyed the question into her ppc.

"Second question," Alex said, "Who is responsible for the scarlet A? Did Arlo paint the A on the bust, and if he did where is the money? Either Arlo gave access to the freezer to someone or he painted the A himself."

Harriet keyed in the questions and looked up. "Between Richard's story about the Scarlet Letter and Valerie accusing Adelaide of being a whore I think we can safely assume that the A stands for Adulteress. Would you agree?"

Alex drummed his fingers. "Yes. It seems the most likely explanation. Payson told me that Adelaide was considered very beautiful when she was younger and often accompanied wealthy men to parties and events. Apparently she had a reputation back then. Payson called her 'popular'. I think it was his polite way of saying Adelaide slept around."

Harriet's mouth dropped open. "Payson knew Adelaide Pelookie?" she asked in surprise.

"Knew *of* her," Alex corrected. "Apparently some of the men Adelaide dated moved in the same circles as Payson. He says he never dated her himself."

"Off topic, but you know, I have no idea what it is that Payson does," Harriet observed. "For some reason he reminds me of a professor. He's very intelligent and has a presence, like he's used to commanding a room full of students."

"I don't know what he does either, but he has some serious computer chops."

"How do you know that?"

Alex told Harriet about the tech equipment he'd glimpsed in Payson's spare room. "Enough about Payson. Back to our two little murders. Who would want to publicly shame Adelaide Pelookie?"

"A jealous wife," Harriet answered promptly. "Like Valerie. Or Richard's wife if he also had a fling with Adelaide. Have you spoken with Richard's wife yet?"

"Only briefly the night of Adrian's murder. I'm also curious about why Richard asked to meet with you and then told you the story about the Scarlet Letter. That sounds—" his eyes narrowed. "Where did you get those bruises on your arm? They look like fingerprints."

Harriet rubbed the arm that Richard had grabbed. "It's not important."

Alex was out of his chair and at Harriet's side before she finished speaking. He cupped her elbows and lifted her to her feet.

"It *is* important," he said. His blue eyes bore into hers like lasers. "It's important to me. I'll not have anyone hurting you."

Despite the softness of his voice Harriet could hear the anger in it. She didn't want Alex to risk his job by confronting a guest on her account so she patted his chest gently in an effort to soothe him.

She felt the muscles in his broad chest and the strength in his hands holding her elbows. All that masculine power and beauty clouded her minded for a moment. She swallowed and focused.

"Really, it's nothing, Alex. Richard didn't realize he was

holding me hard enough to cause bruising. He was upset at the time. Let it go."

Alex released Harriet's shoulders. "Richard again. I think it's time I had a serious sit down with Richard Pelookie *and* his wife."

CHAPTER NINETEEN

Before Alex could request that Richard and his wife come in for an interview, Fox contacted Alex on his link and told Alex he might have something. He asked Alex to meet him in the security office lobby.

Alex hurried out to the lobby, curious to learn what Fox's second interviews with the kitchen staff had turned up. To Alex's surprise, Fox had brought one of the female kitchen workers with him. His curiosity piqued, Alex felt the first stirrings of hope that they might get down to the bottom of the murders.

Fox introduced Alex to Ellen Sue Mayberry and asked Alex to join them in Interview Room One. Alex held the door for them and nearly smiled when he caught the excited gleam in Fox's eyes. Something was definitely up.

Fox took the seat next to Ellen Sue and Alex settled on the opposite side of the rectangular wooden table. Even though the interview room was far nicer than the ones either man had used in their previous jobs, there was no question that they were there on serious business.

The witness obviously knew this. She laced shaking fingers together and studied the table top.

Meanwhile Alex studied Ellen Sue.

The kitchen worker wore a blue chef's coat that flattered her peaches and cream complexion. Like many cooks she had a chunky build. Her round face was rather plain and not helped by the fact that she wore her brown hair pulled tightly back and gathered into a small bun at the nape of her neck.

Ellen Sue would blend into a crowd except that her hazel eyes gleamed with intelligence. Alex put her age in her late twenties.

It was time to play good cop.

"Can I get you something to drink, Miss Mayberry?"

"No, thank you. I'm good."

Her voice was low and husky, pleasing. Alex watched those telltale hands relax.

"Alex, Ellen Sue approached me after I left the kitchen today. She says that she was afraid to speak to either of us earlier but now she has something she wants to tell us. Is that right, Ellen Sue?"

"Yes."

Alex gave her an encouraging nod. "What is it that would you like to tell us, Miss Mayberry?"

Ellen Sue reached into her chef's coat pocket and pulled out a small, velvet box. She slid it across the table toward Alex and nodded at it.

He took the box and opened it. Inside was a sparkling diamond ring. Not the largest jewel he'd ever seen, but not a cheap one either. He snapped the box shut and slid it back toward Ellen Sue.

"Congratulations."

"My fiancé Donny gave me that ring yesterday," she told

them. "I was excited, you know?" She looked at Alex expectantly.

"Sure," he answered with a nod. "It's exciting to get engaged. A big step toward your future." Where was she going with this? He looked at Fox for a clue but Fox's expression was neutral.

Ellen Sue gave a curt nod. "Yes, it is a big step. A very big step. I never expected to find someone to love me and want to marry me, you know?"

She didn't wait for Alex to answer. "Donny and me have only been dating for about three months. When he proposed last night and gave me this ring I about fainted from shock. It's really quite beautiful," she added wistfully.

She slid the box back toward Alex. "The thing is–" she took a deep breath, let it out. "The thing is, there's no way Donny could afford a ring like this. He doesn't have family money or anything to sell to raise cash. Which means he either stole it or he found a large wad of cash somewhere. Which he then stole."

She pushed the ring box even closer to Alex. "Either way I can't keep the ring. You can see that, right? It just wouldn't be right to keep it. I love Donny, but–it would be like *I* was the one who stole if I kept this ring."

Ellen Sue sat back in her chair and crossed her arms over her chest. A little deflated and sad now that she'd said her piece. The yearning look she gave the ring box said it all.

"Where do you think Donny might have found the money?" Alex probed. "Do you think he stole it from a guest?"

Ellen Sue shook her head. "No. I think he took it from Arlo." Her face paled and she swallowed.

"I didn't want to believe it, but the day before he died, Arlo was bragging about making a pile of extra dough and paying back the money his uncle had loaned him. Donny asked Arlo if he needed any help because he was interested in making some extra money too."

Tears began to stream down Ellen Sue's cheeks. "I didn't know at the time that Donny was planning to ask me to marry him. We've only been dating three months," she repeated. "That's too soon."

Fox patted her on the shoulder. "I'm going to get you something to drink, Ellen Sue. Alex and I just have a few more questions, then you can get back to work."

He poured Ellen Sue a glass of iced tea from the room's refreshment center and set it in front of her.

"Alex, could I see you outside for a minute? Ellen Sue, we'll be right back."

The two men left Ellen Sue in the interview room and stepped away from the door.

"What do you think?" Fox asked in a low voice.

"I think we may have a line on Arlo's killer," Alex answered. He related his earlier conversation with Harriet about there being two killers at work, not one.

"If Ellen Sue is telling the truth it sounds as if Donny knew Arlo had a wad of cash on him and saw an easy way to afford a ring for his girl. I'm going to go pick Donny up now. Keep Ellen Sue in the room until I have Donny in Interview Room Two, then you can let her go. I don't want him to see her. I'll tag you when I have him."

Alex had no trouble locating Donny. Armed with Ellen Sue's description, he found the skinny sous chef chopping vegetables under Chef Fritola's watchful eye and requested his presence at the security station without telling Donny why.

He tagged Fox as soon as he had Donny sequestered in the second interview room and waited for Fox to see Ellen Sue out and join them.

"What's this about then?" Donny asked. Beneath his arrogant swagger, Alex detected nervous tension.

Fox walked in a moment later and set the ring box on the table in front of Donny. Donny's eyes widened. He snatched up the ring box and glared at Fox.

"Where'd you get this?" he demanded. "Did someone steal this from Ellen Sue? I want the bastard thrown in jail."

"Actually we were wondering where you got the money to buy such a beautiful ring on your salary, Donny." Alex spoke before Fox could answer. He watched the chef's face pale and his muddy brown eyes dart around the room. His gut told him that they had found Arlo's murderer.

It took them only twenty minutes to get a confession from Donny. Desperate to come up with the money for a ring worthy of his girl, Donny had tried to convince Arlo to let him help with the side project Arlo had going.

After Arlo refused Donny's offer of help, Donny followed him that night. He watched Arlo meet with a woman outside the kitchens and let her into the freezer. Five minutes later the woman left after giving Arlo a roll of money.

Donny hung his head. He didn't know what came over him. Only that he was desperate to impress Ellen Sue with a ring that was worthy of her.

He had grabbed a knife from one of the work stations and forced Arlo to take off his shoes and walk back into the freezer. Then he used the knife to hold Arlo off while he quickly disabled the alarm.

"I held the door from the outside so he couldn't open it," he explained. He waited three hours before letting himself back into the freezer, took the wad of money and Arlo's i.d., and fixed the door handle so people would think Arlo's death had been an accident.

"Why did you make Arlo take off his shoes?" Fox asked.

Donny shrugged. "I don't know. It seemed like a good

idea at the time. I was hoping you'd think Arlo was on drugs or something. Out of his gourd, you know? Who would walk barefoot into an industrial freezer? Only someone who was whacked."

Alex stared at the sous chef and felt sadness mixed with anger. An innocent young man had died because Donny wanted to buy his girl a ring and wasn't willing to scrimp and save for it. He forced down the anger that threatened to fill him.

"Donny, did you look at the ice sculptures when you were inside the freezer?" Alex asked.

"Sure did. Chef did a beautiful job on them." Donny shook his head. "Too bad one of them was messed up with that red A. Chef didn't like that."

A half hour later Fox and Alex stood together outside the interview room. They'd left Donny weeping when he'd heard that Ellen Sue had turned him in and refused his ring.

"The hell of it is," Alex said, "if Donny had left the door handle alone and not taken Arlo's shoes, we would probably have written off Arlo's death as accidental."

"We would have checked the emergency button," Fox pointed out.

"Yes, but all we found was a loose wire. That alone wouldn't have been enough to make us suspicious."

"True." Fox sighed. "People can be so messed up. What's next, bossman?"

"Next we need to figure out why Adrian Pelookie painted a scarlet A on her mother's ice sculpture," Alex answered. "Maybe then we can figure out who killed the woman."

"Do you want me to contact the mainland and arrange for a resort shuttle to deliver Donny to the Miami cops?"

"Yes, and I want you to go with him. Stay the night. I'll inform Chef Fritola that we've found his nephew's killer."

Fox went back into the interview room to cuff Donny and take him to the island's shuttle pad.

Alex headed to the kitchens to find Chef and tell him about Donny. He hoped that learning who had killed his nephew Arlo would help, but in Alex's personal experience it really made no difference.

The loved one was still forever lost to those who remained behind.

Sometimes people sucked.

And then there were those like Harriet who tried to make the world a better place despite their own rocky path.

He held onto that thought while he went looking for Chef.

CHAPTER TWENTY

Alex had no intention of heading to Harriet's when he went for an evening run. But the sadness that lingered within him after he had informed Chef Fritola that Arlo had been killed for an engagement ring wouldn't go away.

He needed comfort and somehow his feet found their way to Harriet's door.

Arlo's death had reminded him of his older sister, Alyssa. He had become a cop and ultimately a murder detective because of her. Alyssa had been killed by a mugger on her eighteenth birthday. The mugger wanted Alyssa's new sneakers for his girlfriend and hadn't given Alyssa a chance to remove them. He'd simply knifed her and taken them, leaving her barefoot and bleeding on the sidewalk.

Eighteen years later and Alex could still feel the loss of his beloved sister. All his life he had looked up to her. Four years older than him, Alyssa had been smart, kind, and beautiful–a talented artist with a bright future. She had encouraged Alex to follow his dreams wherever those dreams might take him.

When Alyssa died Alex tossed away the dreams of a young man and devoted his life to putting away the scum who stole others' futures for no good reason. He grew into a man who guarded his heart and never let anyone get too close. Until Harriet Monroe had arrived on the island and snuck beneath that guard.

Alex wiped the sweat from his face with his tee shirt and leaned his shoulder against Harriet's door. Why was he taking such an unpleasant trip down memory lane today? He must be overtired to have let Arlo's death get to him the way it had. The senselessness of it felt like almost too much to bear.

But then—nine times out of ten—most murders could be said to make no sense at all. Yet people continued to kill. That's why he had eventually burnt out as a murder cop and escaped to Resort Island, looking to replace the day-in and day-out ugliness of a depraved humanity with the peace and natural beauty of the island.

He really wasn't fit company for anyone in this mood. Least of all Harriet. She didn't need his darkness.

Alex straightened away from the door and turned to leave.

"Alex! It's good to see you. Have you rung Harriet's bell yet? I know she's in there."

Solly bounded up the step to stand beside Alex. His keen gaze took in the tired lines on Alex's face but he refrained from commenting. He held up a bottle of wine in one hand and a bag of groceries in the other.

"Ring it for me, will you? I'm going to cook dinner for me and Harriet. Join us. There's plenty to go around."

"Thanks, Solly, but I was about to leave. I'm not sure I'm fit company tonight."

"All the more reason to join us then," Solly said firmly. "You need to be with friends. That would be us. You don't even have to talk. Just have some wine and eat."

Alex took a deep breath and let it out. He really didn't

want to be alone. "Thanks. I could eat. And a glass of wine wouldn't hurt."

Solly beamed at him. "Great. Ring the bell."

Harriet opened the door to find the two men she loved most in the world standing on her front step. She smiled and held the door wide open. Solly walked in and headed for the kitchen.

Alex walked in and gathered Harriet into his arms. He buried his face in her hair and breathed in the scent of night-blooming jasmine mixed with an unnamed spice and fresh air that was uniquely hers. Tears pushed at his throat and he swallowed them back. He didn't want to make a fool of himself.

Harriet wrapped her arms around Alex's waist and squeezed. "Rough day?" she whispered against his neck. She felt him nod and swallow several times.

"I'm glad you're here," she told him, and rubbed his back.

She held him tightly for several more minutes until she felt some of the tension seep out of his body.

Alex reluctantly let her go and took a step away. "Sorry." His voice sounded thick. He cleared his throat. "I shouldn't have just shown up at your door like this."

Harriet had never seen Alex looking so down and vulnerable and it worried her. Something must have happened after she had left his office, but she knew that now was not the time to ask. Showing her concern would only make him feel worse so she scowled at him instead.

"You're kidding, right? Don't insult me, Alex. You can come here whenever you want. I'll always be happy to see you. Always. Besides, I showed up at your door at three in the morning and you didn't turn me away, remember?"

She was relieved to see Alex crack half a smile. Despite whatever had been bothering him, he was getting his equilibrium back. When he was solid again she would question him about it.

"Wine's poured," Solly called from the kitchen. "Come keep me company while I cook."

Harriet took Alex's hand and led him back to the kitchen. They sat at her pink granite island and sipped at the chilled white wine.

Harriet and Solly chattered about the beach, about Solly's greenhouses, and about the group of children scheduled to show up in a day and a half while Solly filleted and cooked black sea bass steaks. Harriet got up and made a salad and gave Alex the job of washing the lettuce.

By the time they took their plates onto the lanai to eat Alex felt more like himself.

"Thanks for giving me some time," he said, after they'd cleaned their plates and were settled back with a fresh bottle of sauvignon blanc.

Harriet reached over and took his hand in hers. "Anytime. Do you want to talk about it?"

Alex stared out over the water. The setting sun hung blood red low on the horizon and had turned the ocean red-purple with streaks of gold. Within a few short minutes the orb that made life on Earth possible would disappear and darkness would be instantaneous. Even after four months on the island that instant nightfall surprised him.

He waited for the sun to disappear before he spoke. No lights showed from Harriet's cabin to break the dark, only the billions of stars set in a velvet black sky. Brilliant green phosphorescence tumbled against the shore as waves gently lapped at the beach. The chorus of frogs singing in the mangrove swamp at the southern tip of the island carried on the breeze. A mockingbird joined them with its mimicry.

The faint scent of grilled fish mixed with salt and the

perfume of flowers. He sipped his wine, appreciating the tart, subtle flavors of apple and melon.

Alex felt the rest of the tension leave his body. He squeezed Harriet's hand, then laced his fingers with hers and told them that Fox had found Arlo's killer. Then, without thinking about why, he told Harriet and Solly about his sister Alyssa's murder.

He had never shared that story with anyone before. His sister's death was something he had always held in a tightly closed, secret compartment of his heart.

"What a lousy reason to kill."

To Alex's relief Solly didn't try to tell him how sorry he was for Alex's loss.

"It was a long time ago." Eighteen years. And yet it still felt like it had happened only yesterday.

Harriet squeezed his hand but didn't say anything. He appreciated that she knew there was nothing to say.

Solly passed the wine bottle to Alex to refresh his glass and settled back in the chaise. "So. We now have an eyewitness who saw Adrian Pelookie pay Arlo to let her into the freezer to deface her own mother's ice sculpture. I wonder why she would do that?"

"What if she was sending a message," Harriet said slowly. "Adrian could have heard the rumors about her mother and other men before Adelaide married Bennet."

She warmed to her theory. "Richard Pelookie told me today that Adrian was keen to move up in the family business. What if Adelaide was holding her daughter back for some reason? What if Adelaide didn't approve of Adrian's party girl lifestyle and told her to stop it if she expected to hold a higher position in the family business? That would be like the pot calling the kettle black. It would have angered Adrian."

"Enough to embarrass her mother in front of the entire

family and close friends?" Alex shook his head. "I don't know."

"If Adrian put the A on her mother's bust, she must have known about Adelaide's history." Harriet didn't wait for Alex to agree. "Given Adrian's own outrageous behavior I'm not sure she would have cared about embarrassing the family. She did put the A on the bust, after all."

"But why kill Adrian?" Solly asked. "Everyone apparently knew about the A before the great unveiling–at least the Pelookie family did–and it was gone by then. So why kill her?"

Harriet stared out over the water, thinking back to the party the previous night. "Adrian didn't know the A had been dealt with. I was watching her when she unveiled the busts. She was expecting a reaction and she was angry when she didn't get one."

No one spoke for several long minutes.

"I think I'll question the senior Pelookies again tomorrow." Alex forced some cheer into his voice. "Let's talk about something else. Is everything ready for your kids arrival Saturday, Harriet?"

Even though the conversation moved onto other topics, Alex continued to mull over the puzzle of Adrian's murder with half his brain. Killing Adrian Pelookie made no sense. Murders that made no sense were the most difficult to solve because there were no obvious threads to follow. He needed to dig deeper and find a thread before the family left.

"I'd love to stay longer but I need to get up earlier than usual tomorrow so I'm going to call it a night." Solly stood, leaned down, and kissed Harriet's cheek. He straightened and looked at Alex. "Keep me posted on your progress and let me know if I can do anything to help." A moment later he disappeared into the cottage next door.

Alex still had Harriet's fingers twined with his own. He

gave a gentle tug. She answered by rising and settling on his lap, snuggling against his chest. He wrapped his arms around her and considered how fortunate he was that she had filled the position of public relations director for the resort.

"Thank you."

The words rumbled in Alex's chest beneath Harriet's ear.

"For what?"

"For being here when I needed you. For being who you are. For not spouting platitudes when I told you about my sister. I love you."

Alex lifted Harriet's chin and planted a soft kiss on her lips.

"And I love you." She hesitated, then decided to take a chance. "Would you like to spend the night?"

Alex sighed. "I would, but I can't. I need to dig deeper into Adrian's life, and the lives of her family. I need a thread, something to follow to her killer and I'm running out of time."

Harriet didn't argue. "Don't leave just yet, then. Let's sit here and listen to the waves and the frogs and look at the stars and appreciate what a beautiful gift it all is."

"Sounds good to me."

They sat like that and talked in between silences for another hour before Alex reluctantly took his leave. The urge to tell Harriet about her past had been overwhelming. It felt as if he was keeping an important secret from her, and in truth he was. But Payson had the right of it–they needed to let Harriet enjoy the coming week with her kids.

Then life was going to get very, very difficult for her.

CHAPTER TWENTY-ONE

Later that night following his dinner with Harriet and Solly Alex donned a clean pair of jeans and a tee shirt and headed down to his office after a shower. He felt refreshed and with Harriet and Solly's help had managed to shake off the melancholia that had gripped him after discovering the identity of Arlo's killer.

Mary the droid came alert when he walked through the door, scanned him, and returned to standby mode. Alex unlocked the steel doors that secured the south wing of the security office and waited for the short buzz that let him know they had relocked.

Since his office had no source of outside light it should have been no different being there in the middle of the night than it was in the daylight hours. During his career as a NYC murder cop he had worked through many nights and hadn't thought twice about it because that was part of the job.

But since he had taken up the position of security director on the island he had gotten used to having nights off unless something was happening that required his presence.

Even then, he was usually able to crawl into his bed by one in the morning at the latest. He had grown soft.

Or maybe not soft, he mused as he let himself into his office and flicked on the lights. It was more of a mellowing. He was looking for something different from his life now. He no longer felt the need to hunt killers as if his own life depended on it.

The life of a hard driving murder cop had left room for little else in his life. In the last few months on the island he had felt ready for more. More meant Harriet. Maybe even children if they were lucky.

He pushed away images of happy children with honey colored hair and silver blue eyes and settled in to work.

It was well after midnight, too late to call Payson, so Alex shot off a memo instead telling him about Donny the sous chef killing Arlo so he could buy an engagement ring and outlining the details about Arlo giving Adrian Pelookie access to the busts in the walk-in freezer. He ended it with his assumption that Adrian had painted the scarlet A on her mother's bust the night Arlo was killed for reasons yet unknown.

To Alex's surprise, his link buzzed minutes after sending the memo.

"Payson! I thought you'd be asleep by now or I would have called you to tell you about Donny."

Payson smiled. He was dressed in the loose, Asian-styled pants and shirt that Alex had seen him in earlier, only these were a steel blue that set off Payson's white hair and tanned face. He looked wide awake, his pale blue eyes sharp and intelligent.

"When you get to be my age you'll find that you don't want to waste too much of your life sleeping," Payson told him. "So, there are two killers. Does that make your job easier or harder?"

Alex thought for a minute. "Both. Donny's eyewitness account of watching Arlo let Adrian into the freezer confirms that there's a link between Arlo and Adrian but I know Donny didn't kill her so there's no link between the murders. That means I need to find the motive for Adrian's murder."

"And you're sure that Adrian is responsible for the scarlet A on her mother's bust, even though she tried to make Harriet think someone else put it there?"

Alex nodded. "It's too far-fetched to think that with all that activity around the freezer that night that someone else snuck in and painted the A. Plus, painting the A is the only reason I can come up with for Adrian to pay Arlo to let her inside the freezer in the middle of the night."

"Do you know why she branded her mother with the A?"

"No." Alex sat back in his chair. "But today Samuel Pelookie's wife Valerie told Harriet that Adelaide had slept with her husband Sam. Harriet said Valerie sounded quite angry about it. How recently that occurred–whether it was before or after Adelaide and Bennet were married–we don't know."

Payson looked thoughtful. "Adelaide's wild party girl days were more than two decades ago. I suppose she could still be messing around but keeping it very private. However, if cheating on a spouse was the motive to commit murder, I'd expect Adelaide to be dead, not Adrian."

Alex stretched out his legs and steepled his fingers, tapping them together while he thought.

"Yeah, I agree with you on that. The sleeping around rumors say more about Adelaide's character than Adrian's– although according to Richard, Adrian is following in her mother's footsteps. Still, that feels like a weak reason to kill Adrian."

He recalled the way Adrian had come on to him before

the party and shared it with Payson. "I suppose Adrian might have had a fling with a family member's spouse, but we didn't hear any rumors to that effect when Fox and I interviewed everyone. They all seemed to accept that Adrian was a 'little wild and out there' as one cousin put it, but they all seemed to tolerate her."

"That's not very helpful, is it?" Payson tapped something and Alex realized he was in his spare bedroom using the hi-tech equipment he kept hidden away in there.

Despite his curiosity, Alex didn't ask Payson about what he was doing. Until Payson told him about the equipment it wouldn't be right to bring it up. There were international laws about what people could access and stiff penalties for breaking those laws.

For all he knew, Payson could be breaking the law. If that was the case then Alex didn't want to know about it. He liked and respected and trusted Payson, and he honestly didn't care if the man engaged in unlawful activities–as long as he didn't kill anyone.

"There's another angle to look at," Alex said. "Richard told Harriet that Adrian wanted to move up in the family business. Might be something there if she was stepping on toes, maybe trying to edge another family member out."

"Harriet's ears get bent a lot, don't they?" Payson said with a chuckle. "People seem to open up to her."

"She's pretty special," Alex agreed.

A knowing look came into Payson's eyes. "Patience, son. After Harriet's project kids leave we'll help her. I promise."

Alex sighed and ran a hand through his hair. "I know. I think I'm on edge about it because I'm half terrified of how it will turn out and at the same time I'm anxious for her to get her whole brain functioning properly again."

Alex's mouth twisted into a semi-grimace. "I also have a niggling fear that Harriet might not forgive me for meddling so intimately in her personal business. What she went through with the cult was a huge deal in her life. After the mass suicide it was all anyone heard about in the news feeds.

"The only good thing Harriet's aunt and uncle did was to keep her away from the press. If that head doctor we're taking her to decides to talk to the press it will all make headlines again and the whole world will be focused on Harriet. Again. She'd hate that."

"Don't worry, Alex. I can guarantee that Dr. Stephens won't say a word. You have my promise on that as well. Tell me what your next steps are to find Adrian's killer. I must admit that I'm curious about why she painted the A on her mother's bust. She had to know it would embarrass and probably anger Adelaide. Did something happen to make Adrian act out?"

"You mean some precipitating event?" Alex set aside his worry about Harriet and focused on the current problem. "That's a very good question, Payson. You should be a cop." The men grinned at each other.

Alex opened his favorite law enforcement search engine. Even though he was officially retired from active duty he paid his dues to retain access.

"I'll dig deeper into the family dynamics and Adrian's history, see if anything pops. I'm going to run some more detailed background searches on the three brothers and their wives, including Adelaide. I want to know as much as possible before I interview them tomorrow. Or today, rather."

"Check your inbox, Alex. I did some research since I had some spare time today. There might be enough there for you to work with. You can grab a few hours shuteye."

Sure enough, six new files sat in Alex's inbox. He downloaded the files and sent them to the printer.

"Thanks, Payson. I'll read them before I quit for the night.

I'll keep you posted on whatever I learn so you can pass it along to Mr. Wade."

"I have the feeling that the scarlet A is the key, Alex. Figure out why Adrian painted it and I think you'll know why someone thought she needed to be killed. Good night."

"Good night, and thanks again, Payson."

Alex gathered the printed files and headed back upstairs to his apartment. He might as well read them in bed. Hopefully he'd squeeze in a few hours of sleep.

While he read he kept an ear tuned for a soft knock on his door even though he knew the odds of Harriet showing up again were slim to none. Eventually he turned out the bedside light and folded his hands behind his head to mull over the information in the files that Payson had sent.

The Pelookie Prison Company was on firm financial footing. No surprises there. Off-planet prisons were filled to capacity and more were being built all the time.

What *had* surprised Alex was the fact that the company was not owned equally by the three brothers. Bennet, as eldest brother and CEO, held forty-five percent of the company shares, with thirty-six percent distributed equally among Samuel, Richard, and Adelaide, and the remaining nineteen percent divided among the–Alex did a quick count–fifty-two other members of the family.

Unless Samuel, Richard, and Adelaide pooled their shares with a group of the smaller shareholders, Bennet would always have the voting power. On the other hand, if the majority of the shareholders disagreed with Bennet, they had the power to vote against him.

Since Bennet had founded the company and then brought his brothers in, it seemed like a more than fair agreement. But it did also show that the two younger brothers were not equals in the business. Did they resent Bennet's power? He'd made a note to ask the question during the interviews even though he didn't see how that tied in with Adrian's murder.

It wasn't until Alex had reached near the end of the stock share agreement that he found something that made him sit up and take notice.

Adelaide's shares in the company were contingent upon her remaining married to Bennet. In the case of divorce, half of Adelaide's shares went to Adrian and the remainder were to be added to the family's nineteen percent. Adelaide's position in the company also ceased to exist.

If Bennet predeceased his brothers and Adelaide, his shares were held in escrow until a new CEO was named, with the CEO never owning more than forty-five percent of the company. A complicated series of contingencies and share allotments followed. The last one in particular caught Alex's eye.

In the case that Bennet predeceased Adelaide, she lost all of her shares and also her job at the company.

Alex could understand taking Adelaide's shares in the event of divorce. But why take them if Bennet died before her?

The only reason he could think of was that Bennet was protecting himself from a premature death by taking away any reason Adelaide might have to kill him.

Or that could just be his suspicious murder cop brain at work.

Bottom line, none of it got him any closer to finding Adrian's killer.

Alex rolled over and forced his mind to let it all go. He'd let his subconscious mind work at it while he slept.

CHAPTER TWENTY-TWO

Solly had already left for the greenhouses when Harriet rolled out of bed for her morning run. They usually ran together and shared breakfast before heading off to work, a routine they'd established many years before when they were roommates in Portland.

Monday was the day Solly liked to create new flower bouquets for the various lobbies and restaurants. He took away the old ones, recycled any still-fresh blooms into small bouquets for the staff's personal quarters, and composted the remainder.

On Fridays Solly's team worked on bouquets for the individual rooms and cottages because Saturday was the resort's change over day. Current guests left and new guests came in. In between the coming and going Solly and his team replaced the old bouquets with fresh ones for the newly arrived guests. Because Fridays were extra busy, Solly always went in a few hours early leaving Harriet on her own.

Harriet had no worries about running on the beach alone. She locked up her cottage and lightly leaped over the two steps that separated her lanai from the upper reaches of the white sand. Turning to her left, she headed toward the southern tip of the island.

Most of the resort's guests preferred to use the beach near the hotel, and the serious runners ran the narrow shell road that ran the length of the island, which meant few people ventured down to the southern end of the island.

On a rare few occasions there were times when Harriet had to share the beach.

She hesitated when she saw the guest jogging in front of her, headed in the same direction she intended to run, then decided it was foolish to expect to have the beach to herself every time she stepped out of her cottage.

Not wanting a conversation with a stranger, Harriet controlled her pace so she wouldn't overtake him. Unfortunately, when he turned around he was running right toward her, making a face to face meeting unavoidable.

Harriet tried to ignore the approaching man. She focused on the clear, milky sky and sparkling water, the warm onshore breeze carrying the scent of seaweed and salt, and the soft peeps and cries of the tiny, long-legged shorebirds chasing the receding waves and darting after the tiny creatures left behind.

They were almost upon each other when she let her gaze dart left for a quick look to assess whether the man represented a danger to her, a habit established when she had been a runaway living on the streets of Portland where dangers to a fifteen year old girl abounded.

She recognized the shape of the face and the beaked Pelookie nose and nodded a greeting, not wanting to intrude on the man's thoughts.

The man came to a sudden stop, then bent over with his hands on his knees and wheezed. "I really need more exercise," he gasped.

Harriet ran two steps past him then stopped and turned

back, afraid that if she ran on the man would suffer a heart attack and die. His face was flushed a deep red and he seemed to be having trouble catching his breath.

"Will you be all right?" she asked.

"Yes." He nodded. "Just–give me a moment. Jeezus." He flopped down onto his knees, then sat. To Harriet's relief his breathing leveled out and his color began to look better.

"Aren't you Adrian's Harriet?" The man looked at Harriet and nodded. "Yeah, of course you are. I noticed you at the party. I'm Sammy Pelookie." He held out a sandy hand, noticed the sand and wiped it on his sweat-drenched tee shirt, and held it out again.

Reluctantly, Harriet shook the damp hand and quickly released it.

"I'd better finish my run so I can get to the office," she said. "Nice to meet you, Mr. Pelookie."

"Don't go yet. What if I relapse? You'll feel guilty that you left me on my own when I'm so obviously suffering."

"You look fine to me now, Mr. Pelookie and I really should get going." She turned away, but before she could take a step Sam Pelookie jumped to his feet.

"Call me Sammy. I'll come with you. A beautiful woman like you shouldn't be alone on the beach. There could be dangerous characters around." He gave Harriet a sly wink and gave her body a lingering up and down look.

Harriet clenched her jaw and fought the urge to slug the offensive jerk. There was probably a rule in the employee handbook against striking guests.

"Dangerous like you, you mean?" She didn't try to hide the contempt in her voice.

Sammy. Richie. What was it with the Pelookie brothers and their juvenile nicknames?

Sam gave her what he probably thought was a sexy, "I'm

all man" look. To Harriet it fell far short. She bit back a laugh and shook her head.

"Good day, Mr. Pelookie." This time she didn't hesitate. She picked up a fast jog and quickly left Sam behind. She could feel his eyes on her back. Creep.

Now that she'd met the man she wondered if Valerie's husband made a habit of sleeping around. Adelaide might not have been the only woman he'd betrayed his marriage vows with.

What if he'd also cheated on his wife with Adrian? Harriet and Adrian were close in age and Sam had just tried to flirt with her. Apparently the man had no boundaries when it came to women. Could he have seduced Adrian?

No. Harriet pushed the thought away. It was too incestuous to contemplate. Uncles shouldn't sleep with their nieces. She remembered how horrified she'd been when her own uncle had tried to seduce her. She'd run away from their home when her aunt wouldn't believe her.

She tried to shake off the memories, not wanting to spoil a beautiful morning with thoughts of the aunt and uncle who had taken her in after her parents had died in a tragic accident.

Harriet knew she should be grateful that she had had family to take her, else she would have ended up in an orphanage or a series of foster homes, but the truth was, she felt nothing but an intense dislike for her mother's sister and her husband.

Many of the children coming to the resort the next day would be worse off than she had been after her parents' untimely death. Was she doing the kids any favors by showing them a slice of life that few would ever experience again? Worse, was she setting them up for misery when they had to return to their temporary homes when the week ended?

The mangrove swamp loomed in her path, the end of the beach and the turning point of her run. Because she had started her run later than usual, the air had warmed as the sun climbed and no longer cooled the sheen of sweat on her body.

This morning the light breeze carried smells from deep in the mangrove swamp, odors that were entirely different from the clean, briny smells of the beach. Composting plants and sulfurous, stagnant water mixed with the scent of rotting meat.

Solly had told her the rotting meat smell came from a large carnivorous plant that lived in the swamp and enticed its prey with the promise of dead flesh.

She pivoted and started back toward her cottage, glad to see that Sam Pelookie was a mere speck in the distance. She should tell Alex about her encounter with the youngest Pelookie brother. If Sam had seduced Adrian and Adrian had threatened to expose him that might be a reason to silence her.

Adrian Pelookie hadn't been an innocent, but she still hadn't deserved to die before her time. Harriet had only dealt with the unpleasant side of Adrian. Surely she also had a good side.

The woman had had personal issues to work out, certainly. If she hadn't been murdered Adrian might have worked those issues out, or she might not have. Unfortunately someone had stolen that option from her. Why?

Harriet veered down to the smooth wet sand and picked up her pace until she felt the burn in her calves and thighs. Her bare feet slapped against the firmer wet sand. Water pooled in her footprints as soon as she picked up her feet. She ran hard until she reached the halfway point back to her cottage before slowing into her cool down.

Murder was an ugly thing, no matter what the motive

behind it. No wonder Alex had burned out on his previous job. Chasing down and putting away killers hadn't brought back his sister, and eventually the daily numbers of senseless death had begun to eat away at his soul.

Douglas Wade had saved a good man when he offered Alex the job as the resort's security director. One more thing Harriet needed to thank Mr. Wade for when–or if–she ever got to meet him.

Feeling pensive, Harriet climbed her lanai steps and rinsed the sand from her feet.

She would be glad when the Pelookie clan left the island. Even though none of them had killed Arlo, it was because of them that an innocent young kitchen worker was dead.

Everything was ready for her kids' arrival, leaving her with free time today. She would spend the day doing what she could to help Alex find Adrian's murderer.

Mind made up, Harriet headed inside for a shower and to dress for work.

CHAPTER TWENTY-THREE

Alex greeted his assistant in front of the security office with an extra cup of coffee. He had managed five hours of sleep and was feeling better than he had expected to. Payson had saved him hours of work by providing background data on the principle Pelookies, hours he had gratefully used to grab some shuteye.

"What's the plan?" Fox asked as he took the coffee from Alex. "Thanks for this by the way."

"You're welcome. You'll need it. We are going to try to beard our primary suspects in their lairs and press hard today. They all leave tomorrow and I have no intention of letting Adrian Pelookie's killer get away."

Fox sipped his coffee and gave a contented sigh. "Miss Pelookie's murder is a real skull buster. Who do we start with?"

"We start with the youngest brother and work our way up. Samuel and Valerie Pelookie have a cottage on Black Bart's Cove."

Alex led the way to a nearby resort cart and slid behind the wheel. He preferred faster transportation but the arrival of an attractive resort cart wouldn't alarm Samuel the way the tougher Road Hog might. He wanted the suspects relaxed, at least when he first approached them. It was a game plan he'd employed with great success in the past.

"Hmmm. Valerie's the dame with the bright red moss, right?"

Alex gave Fox a puzzled frown. The man had an unusual love affair with old American jazz slang and often dropped the oddest phrases into conversation. There were times when Alex didn't have a clue what Fox was talking about. Like now.

"Red moss? What the hell is that?"

Fox waved the fingers of his free hand over his head. "Hair. I interviewed Valerie at the party after you found Adrian. Attractive redhead for her age. Black Bart's Cove is the one with the half-sunken pirate's ship, isn't it?"

"Yep. Popular snorkeling spot. All the cove's cottages are filled with Pelookie family members, but Sam is the only brother staying there."

While he drove them to the cove, Alex filled Fox in on the information that Payson had provided without telling Fox where he had gotten the background data.

The pale gray plinth marking the way into the cove appeared on their left. Alex turned down the narrow road, keeping a watchful eye out for wildlife. He was forced to stop for a large frilled lizard sunning in the road. The lizard flared its bright red collar at the cart, then apparently decided it didn't want to do battle and darted into the thick jungle.

"This island is like an alien world," Fox noted. "It's nothing like New England. Not the weather, not the scenery, not the ocean, not the wildlife." He shook his head. "I was looking for different when I came here, but I had no idea just how different it would be." He looked over at Alex. " You know what I mean?"

"I hear you. I like the different." Alex more than liked the different. He embraced it wholeheartedly. Different made it easier to put the past in the past. Different made a new start possible. "Here we are."

Blue water suddenly appeared. The blackened bow and two masts of the sunken ship stood above the water's surface near the mouth of the cove.

"That looks like a real pirate ship." Fox looked surprised.

"It is. Apparently it sunk right there. Legend says that Black Bart was headed back to sea after hiding a load of loot on the island."

"Ooh. Has anyone looked for the treasure?"

"Beats me. You should ask Payson Douglas. He knows more about the island than anyone."

The road followed the curve of the cove behind the cottages. Several resort carts were parked beside every cottage except for one, the one they were headed toward.

Alex pulled onto the square, crushed shell parking pad next to the cottage and climbed out of the cart. Valerie Pelookie came storming around the side of the cottage.

"How dare you leave me stranded, you-you–" She drew up short when she saw Alex and Fox and fisted her hands on her hips.

"What the devil do you want?"

"We were hoping to have a chat with you and your husband, Mrs. Pelookie. Is Sam inside the cottage?" Alex already knew Sam wasn't there. It was obvious that he had left Valerie without a way to get to the main resort.

Valerie scowled at him. "No. My husband is not inside the cottage." She turned away.

Fox moved fast. He fell into step beside her and flashed a smile.

"That's all right. We'll catch up with him later. Perhaps you can give us a few minutes of your time instead? We'd be happy to give you a lift back to the main resort afterward."

Valerie's scowl turned into a wide smile. "Aren't you a sweetheart? I'd love a lift. Why don't you come in? We can chat while I get ready."

Alex swallowed a grin. He had to give Fox credit. The man had a way about him. Suspects rarely caught on that they were being manipulated by Fox. He wisely kept quiet and followed the pair inside the cottage. Valerie disappeared into one of the bedrooms but left the door open.

The cottage was a mess. Clothing had been tossed willy-nilly over the living area furniture, sandy shoes left in the middle of the rug, and dirty dishes were piled on the counter. Alex knew that a pair of housekeepers cleaned the cottages daily. Sam and his wife were slobs.

He moved to the center of the living area but didn't take a seat, nodding to Fox that he should take lead.

Fox moved closer to the bedroom door so he wouldn't have to shout. "We're just finishing up our report on Adrian's murder, Mrs. Pelookie."

Valerie poked her head out the door. "Call me Val. Please. Adelaide is Mrs. Pelookie."

Fox flashed another grin and Valerie smiled back before disappearing again.

"Were you and your husband at the family party the night Adrian was killed the entire time, Val?"

"Yes. Well, no. I left to use the hotel lobby bathroom right before Adrian's big unveiling, but I was back in time to see her lame presentation. I don't like to use those portable toilets. They make me feel so lower class, you know?"

"Ask her if she knew about the scarlet A," Alex said softly.

Valerie came out of the bedroom dressed in a short, form-fitting aqua colored sheath that set off her red hair and showcased shapely legs.

She scoffed when Fox repeated Alex's question and rolled her green eyes. "Adrian told me about the A, of course. She said her mother was going to flip when she saw it."

Valerie pursed her red painted lips. "I don't think Adrian really cared much about how Adelaide would feel when she saw the A."

Since Alex knew that Adrian was the one who'd painted the A on her mother's bust, the lack of concern on Adrian's part didn't surprise him. It did make him wonder again why Adrian had painted the A in the first place. He still felt the A was connected to Adrian's murder.

"Were Adrian and her mother close?" he asked. "How would you describe their relationship?"

"Definitely not close." Valerie slid a few gold bangles onto her slim wrist and shrugged. "They didn't fight. It wasn't like that. They mostly just ignored each other. Can we go to the hotel now?"

Now that Valerie was ready to leave Alex realized he wasn't going to get any more useful information out of her, but he did have one more question.

"When did your husband have an affair with Adelaide?"

Valerie's face hardened. "Who told you about that? That's none of your business."

"When it comes to murder, everything is our business, Mrs. Pelookie. Please answer the question."

"Fine. It was nearly a year after Sammy and I married. When I found out I told Bennet and we confronted Sammy and Adelaide. Satisfied?"

So the affair had happened more than twenty years ago. And yet Valerie was still angry about it according to Harriet. Alex studied her face and posture. Yes, she was still angry, probably even hated her sister-in-law, but he didn't see how Sam and Adelaide's affair could be linked to Adrian's murder.

"Thank you for your time, Mrs. Pelookie. I apologize for bringing up unpleasant memories."

Val stomped to the door. "Fine. Can we leave now?"

The trip back to the main resort was made in silence. Alex could almost feel Valerie fuming in the cart's back seat. Her mood brightened once she saw the hotel.

"Do you think Adelaide's affair with Valerie's husband could be the reason for the scarlet A?" Fox asked as soon as Alex dropped Valerie at the hotel's entrance.

"No." Alex drummed his fingers on the steering wheel. "It happened too long ago. Even if Adrian only recently found out about it—and was trying to make a big deal of it—it doesn't wash. The affair is old history. And Valerie made a point of telling us that she told Bennet and they confronted Samuel and Adelaide, so it was out in the open."

"Maybe Samuel didn't like the fact that Adrian was raking up old history and decided to do something about it."

"Maybe. Let's ask. That's him walking up from the beach now."

The two men left the cart and walked down the shell path to the upper edge of the beach where they waited for Sam Pelookie to reach them. He hesitated a moment when he saw Alex waiting for him, then walked toward them with a determined look on his face.

"I assume you are waiting for me," he said dryly when he reached them. "What do you want?"

Alex decided on a direct approach. "We want to talk to you about Adrian's murder," he answered. "Why don't we move out of the traffic flow and take one of those benches?"

He led the way to a row of silvered teak benches set just above the beach and indicated that Samuel should sit. Fox neatly sandwiched the Pelookie brother between them.

Samuel tried to look down his nose at Alex even though Alex had nearly half a foot on him. "I don't know why you're harassing us. I intend to complain to the resort owner about the way his paying guests are being treated."

Alex smiled. "You do that." It looked as if Samuel had taken a run on the beach. His tee shirt was soaked with sweat and plastered to his round belly. Surprising, since the man looked too soft for the strenuous workout that running in sand afforded.

"We know about your affair with Adelaide Pelookie."

Samuel's eyes narrowed. "Big deal. Not that it's any of your business, but that was decades ago. Water under the bridge and all that."

"Your brother must have been quite upset with you."

Samuel shrugged one shoulder. "Like I said, water under the bridge. Adelaide liked to party in those days. Benny knew what he was getting into when he married her. Is that all you wanted?" He took his foot off the bench and turned to go.

"Not quite. It occurred to me that a man who would cheat on his wife a year into their marriage might also go after someone inappropriate–like, say, a niece?" Alex looked across Samuel at Fox. "Wouldn't you agree?"

Fox picked up the thread. "Absolutely. There's no telling what kind of inappropriate behavior a man who cheats would get up to." He raised his eyebrows at Sam. "Did you seduce Adrian, Sam? Was she going to tell your brother? Maybe get you into big trouble with Bennet? I'd say that was motive for murder."

"That's disgusting and you guys are nuts if you think I'd seduce my brother's daughter. There are plenty of willing young women out there without fishing in the family pool. And I have better things to do than stand here and listen to your crap." He jumped up and stalked off, grabbed their resort cart, and headed up the road.

Alex and Fox remained seated on the bench, watching him drive away.

"What do you think?" Alex asked.

"I think Samuel Pelookie is a sleazy, cheating putz. I'd like him to be guilty, but I think we can cross Sammy and Val off our list of suspects. There's no motive. What do you think?"

"I agree. Valerie has no reason to want Adrian dead, and although hiding an incestuous relationship *could* be motive for murder, I can't picture Samuel seducing Adrian. He sounded genuinely disgusted by the idea."

"As he should. Who's next?"

"Richard Pelookie and his wife, Melody. They're staying in the hotel. Hopefully we'll catch them here."

CHAPTER TWENTY-FOUR

Harriet was still fuming over her run-in with Sam Pelookie by the time she reached her office. She pasted a smile on her face and greeted Jeeves–who most likely didn't care whether Harriet smiled or not since he was a droid–with a breezy "Good morning, Jeeves" as she sailed through the lobby.

Even walking down the cool, cream colored corridor with its bright island murals and view of the pink crushed shell road and the pale stone kitchen building opposite didn't soothe her. If anything, seeing the kitchen reminded her of Arlo and the trouble the Pelookie family had brought to the island.

She needed to vent.

Harriet hesitated at her office door and then headed for Cassie's office instead. A cheerful "Come on in!" answered her knock. Entering a space very different from her own, Harriet greeted her new friend.

"Hi, Cass, I wonder if you have time for me to bend your ear for a minute?"

"Always. Have a seat. I'll be with you in a minute." Cassie

tapped a couple keys on her computer, pursed her lips, and tapped a few more.

Harriet wandered across the room and chose one of the brightly cushioned chairs set around a glass coffee table. She felt a smile tug at her lips as she watched her friend work.

The bright, bold colors the resort's decorator/designer had used in Cassie's office were similar to the colors Cassie chose to wear–they were the colors of the island people.

Where Harriet's office rugs and fabrics were done in softly muted, tropical tones that soothed her, Cassie's office was as vibrant as the tropical blooms found all over the island mixed with the brilliant colors of the island's sunsets. Reds, yellows, oranges, brilliant greens and bright blues combined into a palette of color that somehow blended and worked.

Harriet wouldn't get a lick of work done in that room but somehow it worked for Cassie. She was a ball of tireless energy.

She hadn't known Cassie long. Events shortly after Harriet's arrival had thrown them together and a friendship had blossomed between the two very different women despite the decade difference in their ages.

"Problem?" Harriet asked when Cassie finally stood and joined her.

Cassie poured two glasses of fresh lemonade and handed one to Harriet before lowering her bulk into a chair. Her green and yellow caftan floated and eventually settled down around her. To Harriet's eye the caftan made Cassie look like one of the island's parrots.

"Not a problem," Cassie said. "Just a puzzle." She took a sip of her drink and leaned forward to set it on a round bamboo coaster. "We have two more murders and a big spike in reservations. Coincidence?" She raised her eyebrows at Harriet. "I don't think so."

Harriet took a sip of the cold, tart-sweet drink and shook her head in puzzled wonder. "People are so strange. You'd think that we'd be seeing a flood of cancellations, not an increase in the number of people wanting to visit the resort. I'll never understand it."

Cassie's face split into a happy grin. "You don't have to understand it, dearie. Just tell me you'll add the latest murders to the Mystery Dinner Theatre once they're solved. We're getting a lot of requests for tickets to the dinner theatre along with the reservations. Word's out that seating is limited and the guests want to be sure they have a chance to participate."

"Ghouls."

A warm, husky laugh erupted from Cassie's massive bosom. "I know. Aren't people grand?"

Cassie's expression turned more serious in the next moment. "I want you to give some serious consideration to changing the name of the dinner theatre to 'Destination Death Dinner Theatre'. It has a more macabre sound, it's more personal to the resort, and it plays up what the news feeds are already calling us."

Harriet's first reaction was that "Destination Death Dinner Theatre" sounded tacky and crass. But she was a marketer at heart, and she knew that Cassie was right—the public was riveted by the murders that had taken place on the most expensive resort island in the world.

She also knew the resort's employees wouldn't be offended—they already jokingly referred to the island as "Destination Death".

"I'll think about it," Harriet promised. "I'm not sure about recreating any recent murders though. There could be liability issues there. I'll have to research the legalities. Plus, you have to admit that the first one was a little too personal for both of us. If we continue to only recreate old murders from history however, then the name change shouldn't offend anyone."

Cassie tapped her lemonade glass against Harriet's. "Great. Destination Death Dinner Theater it is. I'll have the tickets changed. Now what can I do for you this morning?"

Harriet sighed. "I'll think about it" was the same as agreement to Cassie. No wonder the resort manager tended to get her way. She simply refused to take no for an answer.

Harriet let the dinner theatre subject drop and told Cassie about running into Samuel Pelookie during her morning run.

"I don't want to tell Alex about it because Samuel didn't really do anything, but he gave me the creeps, you know? He seems to like younger women. What if he tried something similar with Adrian and she threatened to tell her father about it? As oldest brother and president of Pelookie Prisons, Bennet might be able to push Samuel out of the company. Samuel could have killed Adrian to shut her up."

Cassie looked at Harriet's long, slim legs, then frowned down at her own pleasingly plump figure. "You run every morning? No wonder you're built like a gazelle. I could never do that."

"Cassie! That's not the point."

"No, really, I could never do that."

Cassie settled back in her chair , her expression serious. "First off, do not run alone on the beach again. Yes, the resort is mostly safe, but we do have a constant stream of strangers staying here and who knows—maybe one of them has a fetish for beautiful blondes with legs up to her armpits."

Harriet bit back a smile. "You're not helping," she scolded.

"I'm not finished. I think you should tell Alex any, and every, thing you learn about the prison people. Let him sort through it and decide what's important. What happened between you and Samuel on the beach this morning speaks to the youngest brother's character, and it doesn't speak well. Tell Alex."

Cassie's warm brown eyes twinkled. "I don't think he'll mind. Everyone knows our security director is sweet on you. You were seen coming out of his apartment early yesterday morning, by the way. What is it your friend Solly says? Oh, I know."

She leaned forward and waggled her eyebrows. *"Hubba-hubba."*

"Cassie!" Embarrassed that she was seen leaving Alex's place, Harriet felt her face heat. She thought she'd snuck out of Alex's place without anyone knowing. It was galling to be the subject of rumors when all they had done was sleep together.

She set down her lemonade and stood. "I'm leaving now. Thank you for your input." Harriet heard Cassie's rich chuckle behind her as she shut the office door.

Living on the resort island was wonderful in almost every way, but it was next to impossible to keep a secret there. Everyone paid attention to what was going on around them, and everyone was only too happy to share what they saw or heard with others.

She was about to open the door to her own office when it struck her that working in a family business might be very similar to working on the island. Maybe the younger members of the family and firm noticed things that the older members thought were private. Or secret.

Turning away from her door, Harriet hurried back out to the lobby. "I'll be back in an hour or so, Jeeves, if anyone is looking for me." She didn't wait for answer.

The temperature had climbed to the island's usual low to mid eighties. A soft offshore breeze carried the perfume of jungle blossoms and lush greenery. It still amazed Harriet that when the breeze blew onshore she smelled the ocean and seaweed, and when it blew offshore she smelled the rich perfume of the jungle.

She supposed the breeze was the same on the Maine coast, but she had only really noticed when it carried the smell of rotting baitfish from the wharves across the Portland peninsula. It pleased her to know that she was growing more aware of her surroundings.

She had seen the Pelookie teens on the beach every morning. Hopefully they'd be there that morning as well.

Grateful that she'd chosen to wear capris to the office, Harriet dug her trainers out of her backpack and started to swap them for her heeled sandals but then changed her mind. The teens would be barefoot. If she wore shoes they'd look upon her as an elder, one of their parents' generation. Perhaps going barefoot would make them more comfortable talking with her.

Slinging her pack onto one shoulder, Harriet headed down to the beach. The area in front of the hotel was busy but not crowded. The resort was careful to limit the number of guests so that no area of the island ever felt crowded.

Couples walked together or sat side by side on brightly striped resort towels laid over teak loungers. Three lone adults stood ankle deep in the water, gazing toward the horizon and sipping from go-cups from the hotel lobby.

What were they thinking about? Work, problems at home? Their futures? Harriet avoided disturbing them, moving to stand a short ways off while she waited for the Pelookie teens to show up. The cool, wet sand felt slightly abrasive on her feet. She dug her toes in and enjoyed the feeling.

She wished she had grabbed a tube of water from her office but she didn't want to go back and risk missing her quarry. Fortunately she didn't have long to wait. The Pelookie teens came running down to the water talking and laughing, just as they had done every morning since their arrival.

Harriet smiled at them. "Good morning. I couldn't help but notice how much fun you all seem to be having here. I'm Harriet Monroe, the resort's director of public relations. I wonder if I might have a few minutes of your time?"

She had decided not to approach the teens with direct questions, figuring it would be better to ease into the conversation.

"Sure. How can we help?" The speaker was the largest, and probably oldest, male of the group. He had the prominent nose and dark hair that marked him as a Pelookie.

"Well, I've seen you here at the beach every morning with your boogie boards and skimmers. I take it you all like water sports?"

A chorus of yeahs and laughter. Harriet nodded.

"I have a group of underprivileged kids coming in tomorrow and I wonder what you think they might enjoy most. I'm sure none of them have ever seen an ocean before if that makes a difference. Have you checked out anything else on the island?"

"The circus!"

"The amusement park!"

"Snorkeling Black Bart's wreck!"

"Fishing!"

"Sailing! Jet ski!"

"Eating!"

Everyone laughed at the last one. Harriet laughed with them. "It sounds as if between you all you like everything. That's good to know. It means we're doing our job."

Now came the tricky part.

"I was responsible for the family party so I had to be there. I'm very sorry about your aunt's death."

161

She needn't have worried that they'd be offended. She'd forgotten what ghouls the young could be.

"Someone bashed her head in. There was blood and everything."

The elder boy poked the speaker, a skinny young redheaded boy, in the ribs. "You weren't there, Derek. That's hearsay." He looked at Harriet. "My name's DeShawn. I'm going to be a lawyer and work for the company."

"Pleased to meet you DeShawn. Actually your cousin was mostly right. Adrian *was* hit on the head and there was blood. I helped her put this family vacation together. It's hard for me to believe someone was angry enough about something to kill her."

She didn't say more. She was hoping their natural curiosity and need to be seen as adults would make them talk.

"My mother says Aunt Ree was always playing hard and fast and probably pissed off the wrong person." The speaker, a skinny dark-haired girl, pursed her lips as if she'd bit into something sour. From the way she spoke, Harriet guessed that she'd mimicked her mother.

"Your mother doesn't know what she's talking about," DeShawn scoffed. He turned to Harriet. "Aunt Ree liked to have a good time, but my dad says she also worked hard so she could get away with it. Aunt Ree was upset about something. I heard my mother tell my dad that Aunt Ree went to see my grandfather the week before we came here. They were in his office for a good hour and it looked like she'd been crying when she left."

Harriet didn't dare push for more. She could see the teens were getting antsy to get to their play. "Thank you for your time and the suggestions for my underprivileged kids. It's wonderful to hear that you're enjoying everything we have to offer."

"Especially the food!" Several of the cousins laughed and poked the young, slightly round speaker.

Harriet smiled at them all. "Enjoy the remainder of your stay. Go have fun. I've held you up long enough."

She watched them run off, whooping and laughing. She had never been that carefree. What did it feel like not to have any worries because you trusted the adults in your life to take care of everything for you?

She didn't know if she'd learned anything important from them or not. The news that Adrian had been upset about something was interesting but probably irrelevant. She'd have to look at the guest list and find out which elder Pelookie was DeShawn's grandfather.

It was time to track down Alex and tell him about her morning encounter with Sam Pelookie and the tidbit of information that DeShawn had dropped.

Unfortunately Alex's droid Mary informed her that Alex was not in the building. Would she care to take a seat and wait?

Harriet declined the invitation. She had work of her own that she needed to get to. She tagged Alex on her link but he still wasn't picking up so she left him a brief message asking him to tag her back when he was free.

CHAPTER TWENTY-FIVE

Alex and Fox found Richard Pelookie and his wife Melody in their hotel suite. Richard answered the door still dressed in one of the resort's blue robes. He frowned at the men but didn't invite them in.

"You have news for us?"

"Not yet, Mr. Pelookie," Alex answered. "We have a few more questions for you and your wife. May we come in?"

Richard looked back over his shoulder. "Get dressed, Mel. We have company." He waited a moment, then opened the door.

"This is an unusually early hour to interrogate someone, Mr. Hayes. You must know that you have no legal standing and I don't have to let you in. I'm only cooperating because I want Adrian's killer caught."

Alex gave him a brief nod. "We appreciate your cooperation. I'd like to wait for your wife to return before we begin."

"As you wish."

Alex looked around the space. There were four penthouse suites on the hotel's top floor, all one bedroom with private spa bathroom, a spacious living/sitting room with fireplace, and a well stocked kitchenette. Floor to ceiling windows in Richard's suite sitting room opened to a wrought iron balcony and let in the morning light with a view of the beach and sparkling turquoise water.

A pale teal, deep cushioned couch and two darker teal cushioned chairs set on a cream and white oriental rug faced the windows. A small table in front of the end window held the remains of a half eaten breakfast. Like the rest of the resort's guest quarters, the suite managed to combine homey with elegant.

Richard walked away and returned to a still steaming cup of coffee on the table, leaving Fox to close the door to the suite.

Alex felt no guilt over interrupting the couple's morning meal. He needed answers and it was far easier to beard the family in their dens than to chase them all over the island.

He stepped over to the windows and looked down on the beach, hiding a smile when he saw Harriet standing at the water's edge talking to the Pelookie grandchildren. He had no doubt she was fishing for information. Clever girl.

The children ran off and Harriet headed back toward her office. Alex decided to catch up to her when he finished with Richard and his wife to find out what Harriet had learned.

"You could have warned us you were coming, Mr. Hayes." Melody Pelookie entered the room. She was the plainest of the Pelookie wives, with brown, curly hair and intelligent gray eyes set in an ordinary face, but she had an attractive down-to-earth air about her that Alex found lacking in her privileged sisters-in-law.

He studied Melody for a minute while he contemplated the differences between the elder Pelookie wives. Was it Melody's lack of arrogance compared to Adelaide, and her lack of self-absorbed drama compared to Valerie that he liked? Both of those, he decided, plus her obvious intelligence.

Melody Pelookie was solid. What you saw was who she was.

"Thank you for speaking with us at this early hour," he said. "I apologize for interrupting your breakfast but we are rather short of time if we're going to have any chance to catch your niece's killer."

Melody took one of the chairs. "Have a seat, gentlemen, so I don't have to crank my neck to see you."

Alex moved the other chair so it faced the couch and Melody's chair. He wanted to be able to see their faces when he asked his questions. It was common knowledge that body language accounted for the brunt of human communication, not words.

Fox wandered over to the table, turned one of the wooden chairs around and sat.

Richard hesitated, then took a seat on the end of the couch closest to his wife. He reached for her hand but she kept her own clasped in her lap, ignoring the gesture.

Interesting. Alex wondered whether the strain between the couple was recent or long term. He waited a beat, then began.

"Mr. Pelookie, you've spoken to the resort's director of public relations several times this week--"

"Twice. I've spoken to her twice. Let's be accurate."

Alex inclined his head. "Very well. You've spoken to Miss Monroe twice. The second time you spoke to her you told her that Adrian wanted to move up in the family business. Can you tell me more about that?"

Richard crossed his legs and clasped his hands around his upper knee. "Adrian was ambitious. There was nothing unusual about it. It's a family trait."

There was a soft snort from Melody. Alex let it go for the moment.

"She felt that since my brother Bennet was president and CEO of Pelookie Prisons that as his only child she should be groomed to succeed him when he was ready to retire."

"Did your brother agree?"

Richard wagged his head. "Ben wanted Adrian to show him she was serious about the company. He didn't care for how she carried on in her private life. Ben felt that others wouldn't give her the respect a CEO needs in order to run a company unless she toned down the partying and serial dating."

"Was there anyone in the family who might feel threatened if Adrian moved into the position of CEO? What about you and Samuel? Did either of you feel that you should be next in line?"

"Did I feel threatened enough to kill her? No. I don't want the headaches of Ben's job, and I don't think Sammy does either. We like the perks of our positions but don't want any more responsibility than we already have.

"Nor do I think anyone really believed that Ben would step aside and put Adrian in his place. Adrian was driven, but she was too volatile–she didn't have the right temperament to run the family business."

Alex thought about that for a minute. Richard's words rang true. It seemed that the business line of inquiry was leading nowhere. Alex looked at Fox and raised an eyebrow, a sign that Fox should take over the questioning.

"If Adrian's murder wasn't related to the family business, can you come up with any other reason someone would want her dead?"

Richard spread his hands. "No. Killing Adrian makes no sense."

"What about the business with the scarlet A on Adelaide's

bust?" Fox asked. "We know that Adrian put it there herself. Why would she do that?"

Richard looked uncomfortable for the first time. His gaze shifted from Fox and Alex to out the window.

"I'm sure I don't know what was in Adrian's mind." He unclasped his hands and began to drum the fingers of his right hand on the arm of the couch.

Fox pressed. "You told Miss Monroe a story–something about a Puritan adulteress who was punished by being forced to wear a scarlet A on her dress. Did I get that right?"

Richard gave a curt nod and pressed his lips together.

"I can't help but wonder why you told Miss Monroe that story."

Fox waited. Richard continued to stare out the window, then he spoke softly.

"I told her the story because of that stupid red A that Adrian painted on Adelaide's ice sculpture. The girl just couldn't leave things alone. I thought–I don't know what I thought. I wasn't thinking right when I told the story of The Scarlet Letter to Miss Monroe. It was stuck in my mind. I should have kept my mouth shut."

"Adrian couldn't leave what alone, Mr. Pelookie?" Alex asked. "What was Adrian trying to stir up? We know that Adelaide was considered a party girl when she was younger, before her marriage to your brother Bennet. Why would Adrian rake all that up now?"

"Because she'd recently learned something that shook her up." Melody spoke before her husband could answer.

Alex turned his attention to her. Her face had paled but for two small bright spots on her cheeks.

"Mel. It's none of their business." In contrast to his wife, Richard's face had flushed beneath his tan.

Melody turned a cold look on her husband. "How do you know that, Richard? They're trying to find out who killed your daughter. You should be helping them any way you can."

"Melody!"

"Too late. Cat's out of the bag."

Alex frowned at the couple. "I thought Adrian was Adelaide and Bennet's daughter."

Melody turned her head away from her husband to look at Alex. Her gray eyes were steady, their expression a mix of sorrow and anger.

"You're half right. Adrian is–was–Adelaide's daughter. Adelaide and Richard's. Turns out the oh so classy and arrogant party girl was sleeping with all three brothers, hoping to snag one and secure her position in society. She found out she was pregnant and told Bennet the baby was his since he was the brother with the most money and power. My brother-in-law is a good man. He believed her. He did the right thing by Adelaide and married her."

"You knew about this all along?" Alex asked Richard.

Richard shook his head. "No. I didn't know that Adelaide was sleeping with my brothers too. I found out the week before we came to the island that Adrian was mine. She showed up at our house and confronted me in my study. She'd had a DNA test done for something else–looking for cancer markers, I think she said."

Richard looked at Fox and Alex. "A CEO needs to be able to show a board of directors that they have a clean bill of health," he explained. "So getting a DNA profile is standard." He stopped speaking and ran a hand over his hair before letting it drop in his lap.

"I had no idea," he continued softly. "She showed me the test results. I was her father and Ben was her uncle. She wanted to know how that had happened."

"What did you tell her?" Fox asked.

Richard looked at his wife and swallowed. "The-the

timing was awkward. I was engaged to Mel at the time you see. I told Adrian that I'd had no idea her mother was pregnant until she married Ben and he announced it. Even if I'd known, the father could have been any one of us—or someone else for that matter. I had no idea who else Adelaide was sleeping with at the time."

No one said anything for several long moments. What Richard hadn't come out and said was painfully obvious—he'd been cheating on his fiancé Melody with Adelaide. No wonder she felt angry and sad. Richard had betrayed her before they'd even married. How many times since?

"What was Adrian's frame of mind when she left your house that day?" Alex asked. "Angry, resentful? Did she want to confront her parents?"

"She was understandably upset," Melody answered. "I spoke to her when she left Richard's study, asked if there was anything I could do to help. Of course I didn't know what the problem was at that time. She told me I needed to have a heart to heart with my husband, and slammed out of the house."

"I hadn't seen or spoken to her since that day in my study," Richard said. "She avoided me at the office the rest of that week and here on the island. I'm guessing the scarlet A was Adrian's way of letting everyone know about her mother. She wanted to humiliate her mother the way she felt humiliated."

"Do you know if she spoke to her father about it?" Alex looked from one to the other. Melody shrugged. Richard shook his head.

"I have no idea, but if I had to guess I'd say no. Ben would have said something to me. He would hate knowing he'd been made a fool of and used, and Adelaide definitely made a fool of him."

"And used him," Melody pointed out.

"She used all of us." Richard sounded bitter. "To answer your question, Mr. Hayes, I don't think they'd be here together if Ben knew the truth, so I'd say no, he doesn't know."

"Thank you for your time and your honesty." Alex stood and looked down at Richard. "I'm sorry for your loss. Losing a daughter, even one you've only recently discovered, has to be hard. I'll be in touch again before you leave the island."

Waiting until they had exited the hotel, Alex asked Fox for his thoughts.

"I think that Richard and his wife have some serious weight to wade through and I think we need to talk to Adelaide and Bennet Pelookie, and find out if Bennet Pelookie knew the truth."

For once Alex didn't have to ask Fox to explain what he meant. It was obvious that Melody and Richard Pelookie had some serious "weight" to deal with. "I agree."

Alex pulled up his link and dialed the elder Pelookie couple's suite. "No one's answering. Check with the concierge and see if she knows what they were planning to do today."

While Fox set off to talk to the concierge, Alex checked his messages and found one from Harriet, but she said only that she'd try tagging him again later.

They were closing in on the reason for Adrian's murder. He could feel it in his gut. That meant that they were closing in on her murderer as well. If only they could wrap it up before everyone left in the morning.

CHAPTER TWENTY-SIX

Harriet decided to return to her office after Mary told her that Alex was out of his own office interviewing Pelookies. Once there she grabbed the latest footage she had shot of the circus and began to scroll through it, looking for the money shots for a new ad, but her heart wasn't in the project. Thoughts of Adrian kept intruding.

According to DeShawn, something had upset his aunt. Something to do with DeShawn's grandfather.

She set aside the circus footage and pulled up the resort's guest list plus the notes she had made on them so she could keep the Pelookie family straight. DeShawn was the son of Andrew and Marta Pelookie. Andrew was the son of . . . Richard Pelookie.

Seeing the name made Harriet frown. Richard Pelookie had approached her twice. Both times he had shared information about Adrian. The first time they had talked Richard had told Harriet the story of the scarlet letter. Why?

She tried to think back to that first conversation. He had intentionally approached her. In fact, he had called her and asked to meet. She realized that he had approached her looking for information. He had asked about the red A on Adelaide's bust, told her that he'd heard a rumor about it.

He'd also said that everyone knew about the ice sculptures, but apparently no one knew about the red A until Arlo had been murdered.

Harriet pushed back from her desk and kicked off her sandals. She began to pace around her office, thinking. Richard had told her the story after Harriet asked him why someone would put an A on Adrian's mother's ice sculpture.

Later he had intimated that Adelaide had earned the A the same way the woman in the story *The Scarlet Letter* had.

If Arlo hadn't died, no one would have known about the A and Adrian would have had her shocking reveal at the family party. Just as Alex had been saying all along, the A was important.

Harriet knew that Adrian had painted the A herself. For some reason she had wanted to embarrass her mother.

Harriet stopped by the lanai doors and looked out. A familiar figure was walking up from the beach toward her office building. Even though Harriet had only met Adelaide Pelookie once–the night of the party when Adelaide had been dressed in a designer gown–the woman was easily recognizable even dressed in the slim white capris and a peach tank top she wore on the beach.

Adelaide noticed Harriet watching her and waved. She veered away from the office entrance and headed for the lanai instead.

Maybe this was a good opportunity to glean a little more information for Alex. Harriet opened the doors and invited Adelaide inside.

"I'm so glad I caught you," Adelaide said, as she declined a glass of mango juice from Harriet. "With everything going on

I'm not sure Bennet remembered to thank you for doing such a wonderful job organizing the family vacation week and the party."

"It's not surprising under the circumstances," Harriet assured her. Poor Adrian. Even the dead woman's mother referred to Adrian's event as a party. "It's kind of you to thank me, but entirely unnecessary, I assure you."

"I believe in giving credit when credit is due," Adelaide said. "I'll make sure Bennet leaves you a bonus before we depart tomorrow."

Harriet was horrified. "Oh, no, please don't do that, Mrs. Pelookie. I was only doing my job. Besides, it took many hands to the care of your family."

"If that's the way you feel about it." Adelaide walked over to the bookshelves and picked up the holo of Harriet's parents. "You look like them," she said.

Harriet resisted the urge to rip the holo from Adelaide's hands. She didn't like having a stranger touch the only memory she had left of her parents. "I really need to get back to work. Thank you for stopping by."

Adelaide set down the holo. "You're right. I should be going."

Harriet headed for the corridor door to let Adelaide out. "Have a safe journey home, ma'am. I hope someone finds out who killed your daughter. I'm sorry for your loss."

"Hmm, everyone says that, don't they? But I wonder how many people actually mean it." Adelaide's expression became veiled. Cold.

"What?" Harriet couldn't believe her ears. What a strange thing to say. "I assure you ma'am, I am truly sorry about Adrian's murder."

"I don't wish to leave that way, my dear. I'll leave the same way I came in, if you don't mind. Why don't you lock that door since you're standing there."

"Why would I lock it?" The woman had grown very strange in the last few minutes. Her next comments only reinforced the strangeness.

"Not very bright, are you? Still, I couldn't take the chance. It's important to wrap up loose ends you see, and you are a loose end."

Adelaide almost sounded as if she was talking to herself. Harriet stood by the door, frozen by the hard expression in Adelaide's icy blue eyes and the stun gun that had appeared suddenly in her hand. Even from across the room Harriet could see that the stunner was set to max. A max stream could kill a man–or a woman–in ten seconds or even less if hit in the torso, depending on the person's physical condition.

"What's going on, Mrs. Pelookie? I'm afraid I don't understand. In what way am I a loose end?"

"Lock the door, Miss Monroe. We'll talk on our way to pick up your friend."

Harriet locked the door. She didn't see that she had any choice.

Adelaide beckoned toward the lanai doors with the stunner. "We're leaving this way, Miss Monroe. I've a cart parked at the back corner of the building. You will drive of course."

Harriet stopped by her desk for her shoes and backpack but Adelaide stopped her. "You won't need them. Everyone will think you went for a walk on the beach as you often do. By the time they realize you are missing I'll be safely stateside and no one will connect me with your disappearance. They'll think you ran off with your friend."

Adelaide pushed Harriet out the lanai door after checking to see if anyone was watching. Unfortunately for Harriet the beach was nearly deserted at the moment. Even the Pelookie teens had vanished and were little more than dark specks far down the beach.

Once they were seated in the cart Harriet asked where Adelaide wanted to go.

"To pick up your handsome friend first. It really is a shame you both had to see me coming out of the hotel."

Everything snapped into focus for Harriet. She turned her head to look at Adelaide. The ugly expression on the other woman's face frightened her more than the stun gun. Adelaide Pelookie was not right in the head. There was no telling what Adelaide had in mind, but Harriet knew she wasn't going to like it.

"You weren't looking for Adrian that night because you thought she might be upset," she said slowly. "You already knew she was dead, didn't you? You were coming out of the hotel . . . Why?"

She thought for a minute. The answer she came up with sent a shiver down her back.

"Because you got blood on your gown. Because you needed to wash your daughter's splattered blood off your hands."

"Yes, Miss Monroe. You are exactly right. And that's why you and your friend have to disappear. No one else realized that I had left the party. I knew that sooner or later you would remember seeing me in a place where I shouldn't have been. It's too bad, really. You are quite good at your job. I hope your replacement can measure up. Turn here."

They had arrived at the greenhouses where Solly was most likely to be.

"I'm sure Solly is out delivering flower arrangements," Harriet said firmly. "You're going to have to forget about him and settle for me."

"Nice try." Adelaide's smile didn't reach her eyes. "I called ahead to be sure Solomon Ayers was on site. He believes I'm here to thank him for going above and beyond."

Before Harriet could think of a reply to make Adelaide give up on Solly and leave, he came out of the center greenhouse wearing a big smile. "Harry! What a treat. Mrs. Pelookie, you really didn't have to do this. We were just doing our jobs."

"Such humility." Adelaide slipped out of the front seat and into the cart's back seat. "You will join your friend in the front, Mr. Ayers."

Solly's brows furrowed until he saw the stun gun trained on Harriet's torso. "What's going on here? Harry, are you all right?"

"Get in the cart, Mr. Ayers before I shoot your friend. Then she will most certainly *not* be all right. In fact she will be dead. Perhaps you cannot see from where you're standing, but I have my stunner set to max. Now stop wasting time and get in."

Solly rounded the cart and climbed into the front passenger seat.

"Drive, Miss Monroe. We're going to the mangrove swamp at the southern end of the island."

Solly reached out to touch Harriet's shoulder. "Harry? You all right?"

"Put your hands on the dash where I can see them, Mr. Ayers. Your friend is all right and will be as long as you do as I say."

"Adelaide Pelookie killed her own daughter, Solly. We saw her coming out of the hotel, remember? She told us she was looking for Adrian because she thought Adrian might be upset about the ice sculptures. She lied. She'd been in the hotel to clean up after bashing Adrian's head in with a coconut."

Harriet turned her head to look at Adelaide. "Why did you kill your daughter, Mrs. Pelookie? What had she done?"

Adelaide said nothing for several long minutes. Harriet turned back to watch the road, wondering if she would get an answer to the mystery of Adrian's murder before Adelaide killed them.

The pink shell road looked every bit as magical as it had on Harriet's first day on the island. The sea sparkled, dolphins leaped in play, seabirds called overhead. She smelled the brine and drying seaweed that came with an onshore breeze.

Shouldn't the day she was going to die be different somehow? Marked by gray skies and angry seas? She cast a sideways glance at Solly and saw a muscle jumping in his jaw, a sure sign that he was angry and ready to lash out. She tried to catch his eye but he was staring straight ahead.

They'd been best friends for so long, saved each other from the horrors of living on the streets, protected each other from the pimps and thugs and drug peddlers who preyed on runaways. How ironic that they should die together in paradise.

"Adrian wanted to rise in the family business," Adelaide said, startling Harriet from her thoughts. "She wanted to take over the CEO position when Bennet retires."

Harriet had nearly forgotten that she had asked a question. She focused her attention on Adelaide.

"Was that so bad?" she asked. She couldn't believe Adrian's ambition was the reason she had to die. Unless Adelaide wanted that top spot for herself.

"No. Ambition is never a bad thing," Adelaide said, her voice sharp. "What *was* bad was that the top job requires a DNA scan to look for genetic markers that are linked to terminal diseases. Adrian jumped the gun and had the DNA test done now instead of years from now when she'd need it. She had a problem with patience."

Solly turned to look at the stun gun trained on Harriet. His usually warm brown eyes were flat and hard.

Please don't try anything, Solly. I couldn't bear to see you hurt, Harriet begged silently.

"Did the test tell Adrian she was going to get a terminal disease?" she asked aloud.

"No. The test told her that Bennet is not her father."

Harriet's breath caught. "Oh. Oh dear. That must have been awkward for you." She risked a look back at Adelaide. Their abductor was scowling at the water but the hand holding the stunner on Harriet was rock steady.

Adelaide turned away from the water and focused on Harriet. "You have no idea, Miss Monroe. Bennet is sterile, but he doesn't know that. I had his sperm tested–tricky, but I managed to do it without his knowledge. I was determined, you see.

"Once I realized my plan to trap Bennet wasn't going to work I slept with both his brothers until I got pregnant, then I told Bennet the baby was his. He married me, of course. I knew he would do the right thing. That's Bennet through and through. He always tries to do the right thing."

Adelaide's tone turned bitter. "He wouldn't have married me otherwise–I wasn't from a good enough family for marriage. It didn't matter how beautiful or smart I was. I didn't possess the right background to be an up and coming CEO's wife. But I had a plan and my plan worked, right up until Adrian took that stupid DNA test."

"So who *is* Adrian's father? Did Adrian know?"

Adelaide shrugged. "It's either Richard or Samuel. I didn't ask her. It didn't matter."

"I bet it mattered to Adrian," Solly said softly. "That was what the bit with the scarlet A on your ice sculpture was about, wasn't it? She was going to tell the whole family what you'd done."

"*Yes*. The little fool. I couldn't let her get away with that. Bennet would have divorced me as soon as he learned that I deceived him. I couldn't let that happen. I'm not going back to being a nothing. It was my good luck that that kitchen worker died and I found out about Adrian's little plan before the party. We're here. Stop the cart and get out."

CHAPTER TWENTY-SEVEN

Alex and Fox stood in front of the security office building after speaking with Richard and Melody Pelookie. The morning was still young but the day had warmed to a comfortable eighty degrees with a soft onshore breeze that smelled fresh and briny.

They had called on Bennet and Adelaide's hotel suite but neither one of the senior Pelookie's had been in. Nor had the couple spoken with the hotel's concierge before leaving. It was going to take time to track them down, time Alex chaffed at.

Alex tagged Harriet on his link but she didn't pick up. Strangely, his call didn't automatically go to message which was unusual. If Harriet had been in the middle of something and hadn't wanted to be interrupted her link should be set to message mode.

He slid his own link back into his pocket with a frown.

"Call the spa and the hotel restaurants and see if you can locate Adelaide and Bennet," he told Fox. "Try the marina as well. I'm going to take a quick run over to Harriet's office."

"Something wrong?"

"I'm not sure. She left me a message, said she had something important to tell me, but now she's not answering and I can't leave her a message. I won't be long. Tag me if you locate either Pelookie and I'll meet you."

"Will do." Fox headed inside the security office to track down Adelaide and Bennet.

Alex jogged over to Harriet's office building and let himself in the front door. A large bouquet of fresh flowers in orange, peach, and yellow sat in the center of the reception counter. He wondered if the reception droid was capable of enjoying them—he knew his own droid Mary would ignore them.

"Good morning, Jeeves. I need to see Harriet. Could you let me through, please?"

"Good morning, Mr. Hayes."

Alex waited for the telltale hesitation that told him Jeeves was scanning his face to verify his identification.

"Mr. Hayes, I have to contact Miss Monroe first and get permission before I let you through."

"That's fine. Tag her. But be quick about it. I don't have a lot of time." An uneasy feeling had crept up on Alex. Dammit. If Harriet was in her office then she would have either answered her link or had it set to message. And if she wasn't in her office she would answer her link, especially after leaving him a message.

"I'm sorry Mr. Hayes, but it seems Miss Monroe is no longer in her office."

"Did you see her leave?"

"No, sir."

Alex's uneasy feeling grew, but before he could insist that Jeeves let him into Harriet's office, Fox tagged him.

"I've located Bennet. He's drinking coffee on one of the benches in front of the hotel."

"I'll meet you there. Don't let him leave." Alex pocketed

his link. "Jeeves, let me know when Harriet returns. It's important."

"Certainly Mr. Hayes. Enjoy the remainder of your day."

Alex didn't bother looking for a cart. He could jog as fast as the carts moved–at least for the short distance back to the hotel. He spotted Fox's red hair immediately. His assistant was leaning against a palm tree behind a bench holding Bennet Pelookie.

Bennet sipped from a go-cup, apparently unaware of his watcher. Alex nodded to Fox and approached the eldest Pelookie.

"Mr. Pelookie. I wonder if my associate and I might have a word with you."

Bennet started, as if he'd been deep in thought, a thousand miles away. "Of course." He indicated the opposite end of the bench. "Have a seat. What can I do for you? Is this about my daughter's murder?"

"It is, yes." Alex took the seat. Fox continued to lean against the palm tree, scanning the beach. Alex realized he was watching for Bennet's wife, Adelaide.

Not for the first time, Alex thanked the lucky stars that had brought Tarbell Fox to the island. Fox had been a good cop before his career had been politically sidelined. Those instincts and training were a boon for Alex.

Alex didn't begin with his questions right away. How to broach a subject that was going to be a shock to the elder Pelookie?

"We've learned a few things since we last spoke with you, Mr. Pelookie," he began. "We understand that your–" Alex hesitated–"that Adrian was keen to move up in the family business. That she had her sights set on taking over your position when you retired."

Bennet nodded. "My daughter had drive and ambition, yes. Whether she had what it took to become CEO of a company the size of Pelookie Prisons remained to be seen, but she showed promise. Now we'll never know."

One of the things that Alex had always found distasteful about police work was having to tell people bad or ugly news about loved ones. He thought he'd left that behind, but it seemed there was no getting away from it. As long as he was hunting murderers there would be secrets to uncover.

It was possible that Bennet Pelookie already knew about the DNA test and had murdered his own daughter, although that scenario was unlikely as no one had seen him leave the party during the critical time.

Alex took a deep breath and asked his question, keeping a close eye on Bennet and his reaction.

"Were you aware that Adrian ordered the DNA test that all company CEOs are required to take to test for any markers that might indicate a predisposition for a terminal illness?"

"I'm well aware of the test, Mr. Hayes," Bennet said dryly. "I had to take it myself, as did my brothers in case one of them needs to temporarily succeed me should I unexpectedly die. I was not aware that Adrian had taken it. I'd say that merely shows that she was serious about her goals."

"Yes. I guess it does. Mr. Pelookie, there's no easy way to ask this. Did Adrian tell you that the DNA test showed that you were not her father?"

The go-cup shook slightly in Bennet's hand, slopping coffee over his fingers. His eyes narrowed and his jaw clamped tight. "Where did you hear that ugly piece of crap, if I may ask, Mr. Hayes? It sounds like malicious gossip to me."

Alex sighed, convinced the man hadn't known. "We heard it this morning from Adrian's biological father–your brother Richard. Apparently Adrian showed up at his house with the test results, demanding to know what was going on. She was quite upset, as you can imagine."

"My brother–Richard? *Richard* is Adrian's father?"

Bennet Pelookie suddenly looked every one of his years. Alex felt bad but plowed forward.

"According to Richard, it was a surprise to him. Adelaide never said a word."

"Adelaide."

Alex saw the exact moment when cold fury replaced shock. The demeanor of a hard-nosed CEO returned and Bennet's expression hardened.

"Finish with your questions, Mr. Hayes. I need to find my wife and brother and have a word with them both."

"Of course. After hearing about the DNA test it occurred to us that Adrian's murder might be connected to the red A she painted on her mother's bust."

Bennet's head whipped around. "*Adrian* painted that A? Adelaide said the kitchen worker was responsible. Why–"

Alex could practically see the wheels turning in Bennet's mind.

"Of course." Bennet nodded and looked back toward the beach. "*A* stands for adulteress. Adrian was lashing out at her mother for keeping secrets. It seems my wife has a lot to answer for." His tone sounded bitter. Bitter and angry.

"Mr. Pelookie, did you kill your daughter?"

"No, Mr. Hayes, I did not." Bennet turned an angry look on Alex. "I loved my daughter. She may be . . ." His voice faltered, then firmed. "She may be my brother's biological daughter, but I raised her. I'm the father that counts. I loved her despite her wild ways."

"One more question, Mr. Pelookie, and then we'll leave you. Did your wife leave the party at any time? Adelaide says not, that she was with you, and your original statement verifies that."

"She left for a short while to look for Adrian after the unveiling of the busts. She thought Adrian looked upset and wanted to check on her. She went to the hotel but when she returned she said Adrian wasn't there. Of course we learned shortly after that that Adrian had been murdered."

Bennet stood. "If you'll excuse me, I need to find Richard and speak with him."

"Do you know where we might find your wife?" Fox asked. They were the first words he'd spoken since Alex had arrived.

"She said she was going to explore more of the island."

"Thank you for your time," Alex said. "And for what it's worth, I am sorry for your loss."

They watched Bennet stride into the hotel.

"I imagine there are going to be some briny words when Bennet confronts his brother," Fox observed. "I'm glad we're going to miss that conversation."

"Yeah, me too. I feel for the man. I think he's essentially honest and strives to live right. He must be feeling a bit gutted."

"So you've taken him off our suspect list."

"Yep."

Fox pursed his lips. "That leaves only one more name."

"Right. Adelaide Pelookie. It fits. She has the strongest motive, the most to lose if Adrian made the test results public."

"And we just learned that she left the party for a brief time. But was it long enough to kill her daughter?"

"It wouldn't have taken long. Adelaide lures Adrian away from the party, maybe tells her they need to talk about the DNA test. As soon as they stepped away from the lights set up for the party they would've been in the dark shadows. Adelaide picked up a coconut, bashed her daughter in the head with it, then hurried to the hotel so if someone sees her she can say that she was looking for Adrian."

"Works for me. Where do we search for her?"

"She took a cart. She could have headed north–"

"–or south."

"Right." Alex pulled his link from his pocket and tried tagging Harriet again. When she didn't answer and he still couldn't leave a message he frowned and slipped the link back into his pocket.

"Still trying to reach Harriet?"

"Something's wrong. I have that itchy feeling."

"Never underestimate that itchy feeling," Fox said solemnly. "Have you checked her office?"

"Yeah. She's supposed to be there but isn't."

"Maybe she decided to take a walk on the beach and left by her lanai doors. She does that now and then."

"True, but she always tells Jeeves in case someone comes looking for her."

"Now *I'm* getting itchy. Let's go peek in her lanai doors. Have you tried tagging Solly to see if he knows where she is?"

Alex set off for Harriet's office with Fox at his side. He pulled his link and tagged Solly again. "No answer. No message."

They stepped onto Harriet's office lanai peered through the glass doors. The office was empty.

"Alex." Fox had opened one of the doors. "Harriet keeps these locked when she's not in her office."

Alex pushed Fox aside and stepped into the empty office but went no further than the doorway. Just in case. Just in case something had happened to her. He forced the thought away.

"Her backpack is here. So are her sandals." Alex looked around the bright airy office carefully, looking for anything out of place. A half-finished glass of juice sat on the bamboo and glass table, moisture pooled at its base. It wasn't like

Harriet to leave a glass like that. She was conscientious about not leaving messes for staff to clean up.

His eyes passed over the bookshelves, then came back.

The holo of Harriet's parents had been turned around so it faced away from the room. The sight made Alex's blood run cold and his pulse kick up.

"Someone else has been here." Alex stepped back outside and closed and locked the door behind him. "Something's wrong. Harriet would never leave her backpack. She takes it everywhere, even when she's walking on the beach."

"Maybe she saw someone in trouble on the beach and rushed out to help."

"No. Someone would have reported it if that was the case." Alex was already headed for the security office and his motorcycle. He pulled his link, tried unsuccessfully to tag Solly again, and slipped it back into his pocket with a disgusted grunt.

"I'm headed to the greenhouses to check on Solly. I'll take my bike. You get the Road Hog and head north. Call me if you find Adelaide or Harriet. Or Solly."

"Right."

They reached the security office at a run and split up.

CHAPTER TWENTY-EIGHT

"If you shoot us, Alex Hayes will know. He'll come looking for you."

Harriet was trying to remain calm but it was taking a great deal of effort. She and Solly were standing near the front of the resort cart after being forced out by Adelaide.

Solly had tripped and fallen to his knees while climbing from the cart, giving Harriet a moment of terror when it looked like Adelaide was going to shoot her friend where he knelt.

Adelaide Pelookie stood near the driver's door, her weapon calmly trained on both of them.

Behind her Harriet could hear the buzz and hum of the insects who made the mangrove swamp their home. A bird trilled sharply and went abruptly silent. A saltwater crocodile bellowed, another grunted. She had yet to see one of the swamp's largest and fiercest hunters, but the thought of them filled her northern-bred heart with fear.

She smelled the rotten egg stench of sulphur and rotting vegetation mixed with the heavy perfume of a carnivorous flower. The mix of strong smells made her stomach feel queasy.

Solly had gone silent and still as a statue. Harriet could feel the tension in his body and hoped he wasn't about to try something foolish. Adelaide didn't seem bothered by the swamp smells at all. She looked positively cheerful, a fact that worried Harriet. Shouldn't the woman be worried about what she was about to do? It should be hard–nearly impossible–to kill another person.

"Never pin your hopes on a man, Miss Monroe," Adelaide told her. "I learned that from my Mama and it was good advice. There won't be anything left for Mr. Hayes to find of you, I'm afraid. Once the saltwater crocodiles smell blood they'll come out of the swamp to look for the source. When they do they'll drag your bodies back into the swamp to eat at their leisure."

Adelaide's smile didn't reach her cold eyes. She gestured with the stun gun. "Move farther away from the cart please. I promise that I'll make this as quick and painless as possible."

"Somehow I can't equate scorched flesh with the idea of painless," Solly said, his tone mocking and sarcastic.

Harriet realized he had maneuvered his foot behind hers. What was he up to? She didn't dare look at him and risk Adelaide noticing.

She tensed, waiting for the stream from the stunner to hit her body and fry her nerves. Despite Adelaide's words she imagined the pain would be extreme, but then she wouldn't feel a thing.

Would she see her parents once she was dead? She wasn't sure she believed in a hereafter where everyone she had ever known reunited, but she realized that she did believe in some kind of hereafter. She wasn't quite ready to find out about it, however.

"I said move away from the cart!"

Two things happened simultaneously. Harriet heard the roar of Alex's motorcycle and Solly jabbed her with his elbow, knocking her off balance. She tripped over Solly's foot and fell backwards. At the same time she saw Solly fling something at Adelaide.

The woman screamed–in anger, not pain–and shot at Solly. Harriet saw the golden yellow stream and heard it sizzle. Solly dove for the sand, landing on top of Harriet.

Alex's motorbike drew closer.

"Dammit." Adelaide let out a string of curses, then Harriet couldn't hear anything except the roar of the bike.

"Solly, get up. I think she's gone. Get up. I can't breathe with you lying on me."

Solly didn't move.

"Solly?" A cold panic filled her.

Alex cut the bike's engine and dropped it in the sand next to the resort cart. He could see Adelaide Pelookie running on the beach, headed north toward the hotel. He'd deal with her later. She wouldn't get far.

"Harriet! Are you all right? Talk to me, dammit."

"Alex, something's wrong with Solly." Harriet's voice shook. "I think she shot him. Adelaide Pelookie. Alex, she killed Adrian. Solly was trying to protect me and I saw the stream and he fell on me–" she dissolved into tears.

Alex knelt beside them and felt Solly's neck for a pulse. He found one, but it was weak and thready. He pulled his link and tagged Dr. Clarke, told her to head for the air shuttle pad. Then he tagged the air shuttle pad and requested their medivac shuttle. Finally he tagged Fox and told him briefly what had happened, then told him to arrest Adelaide as soon as she arrived back at the hotel.

He sat beside Harriet and gently took her hand. She gripped his fingers tightly.

"Can you hang on for a few more minutes?" he asked her.

"Solly took a bad hit and I don't want to move him. The medivac team will be here soon. They'll stabilize him and take him to the mainland. Dr. Clarke will go with him."

"I want to go with him too, Alex." Harriet's eyes were wild, her pupils tiny pinpoints, her face streaked with tears.

Alex squeezed her hand gently. "Of course you'll go. I think he'll feel better when he wakes up if you're there with him."

He felt some of the tension go out of Harriet's body when she realized he wouldn't try to stop her from leaving the island with Solly. He didn't tell her that he wanted her to go to the hospital to be checked out as well.

"He tried to save me, Alex." More tears pooled in Harriet's eyes and she choked back a sob. "Solly got shot while trying to protect me. How did Adelaide get her hands on a lethal stun gun on the island? I thought they were illegal."

"That's a very good question, and one I intend to get the answer to." The gun Adelaide carried was illegal for any civilian to own, issued only to law enforcement and military.

Someone's ass was going to be in a sling, provided they could trace the weapon. Odds were Adelaide had bought the stun gun on the black market on the mainland. She certainly had the funds to pay for one.

Even more troublesome to Alex was the fact that she had smuggled the gun into the resort. They had safeguards and protocols to prevent that from happening. Alex suspected that Adelaide had bribed one of the resort's employees to look the other way. When he identified the culprit that person would be out of a job with no references.

Harriet heard the whop-whop of the medivac shuttle approaching at the same time as movement to her left caught her eye. She turned her head and looked into the jaws of a salt water crocodile sitting just inside the edge of the swamp.

"Alex," she whispered. "There's a crocodile."

Adelaide had been right. The smell of Solly's blood had attracted the monster beast. It looked like something from the dinosaur age, with its thick, knobby hide in mottled shades of brown and olive green and enormous jaws filled with large, curved teeth. Any other time she could appreciate its unique beauty, but not when it was eyeing her for a meal.

Harriet waited for Alex to shoot the croc, or at least stun it, but he didn't draw his weapon.

"Alex?"

"I'm unarmed. Don't move."

Harriet didn't think she had ever felt as frightened as she felt at that moment. She was trapped beneath her dying friend and about to be dragged into the swamp by a hungry beast with more long, sharp teeth than she'd ever seen. She could barely draw a breath she was shaking so hard.

Alex stood and disappeared behind the resort cart.

"Alex?" Surely he wouldn't leave them to be eaten by a crocodile. The man she loved would never do that.

Moments later the motorcycle roared to life. When Alex drove it straight at the crocodile Harriet realized he was trying to scare the creature off. Were the formidable beasts frightened of anything? Between their thick hides and enormously strong jaws the saltwater crocs had to be at the top of the local food chain.

The croc apparently knew that it ruled the swamp. It didn't move. Alex wheeled the bike at the last moment, spraying wet sand into the crocodile's gaping mouth. At the same moment the medivac shuttle arrived and hovered over the scene, its blades beating the air in a heavy whump-whump that vibrated inside Harriet's body.

The combination of the motorbike and medivac shuttle proved to be more than the croc could bear. It turned and slid into the safety of the swamp.

With a silent prayer of thanks for the medivac team's

timing, Alex shut off the bike and rejoined Harriet and Solly. He checked Solly's pulse again. It felt weaker. He didn't tell Harriet. He knew that if Solly died she would never forgive herself.

"Why did Adelaide try to kill you?" he asked, trying to distract her. She took so long to answer he didn't think she knew why Adelaide was going to kill them both.

"Solly and I saw her at the hotel the night Adrian died. It was right after you took Adrian's body away. We were passing the hotel lobby and she was coming out. She asked us if we'd seen Adrian. Said she was looking for her because she thought Adrian was upset about something."

Alex scowled. "And why didn't you mention this to me before?"

"I don't know." It was hard not to feel defensive, trapped on her back with Alex glowering at her. "I'd forgotten that we saw her, I guess. You had just driven off with Adrian's body and here's her mother, concerned about Adrian and asking us if we'd seen her. All I could think about was how I didn't want to be the one to tell Adelaide her daughter was dead."

Before Alex could launch into a full lecture the medivac team swarmed them and nudged him aside. They quickly checked on Solly, their expressions more serious than Harriet liked. Within minutes the team had both her and Solly loaded into the shuttle and they were winging toward the mainland hospital.

CHAPTER TWENTY-NINE

Although Harriet was checked over and released shortly after her arrival at the hospital, Solly was in serious trouble and she refused to leave. She paced the ICU's waiting room floor, alternating between whispering prayers for her friend and scolding him for putting himself in harm's way in a vain attempt to save her. Her eyes burned from holding back tears.

She was the only person in the ICU waiting room. It held four seating areas with separate clusters of scratched, hard plastic, mud green chairs. A vending machine offered tubes of water or flavored fizzy, protein bars, and greasy crisps. The worn carpet of orange and green swirls made her feel ill. Whoever had designed the space had not been thinking of the comfort of tired, distraught loved ones.

Hours passed, and still no one came to tell Harriet how Solly was doing. Alex called her twice, but he was tied up with dealing with Adelaide and couldn't join her.

She was nearly at her wit's end when Payson showed up. He'd exchanged his relaxed island wear for a dark navy tailored suit and tie and looked every bit the businessman.

She almost didn't recognize him, he looked so different from the man she met for Thursday lunches.

"Harry? How is your friend?" Payson placed his hands on her shoulders and peered into her eyes. "Will he be all right?"

"Oh, Payson." Harriet couldn't hold herself together any longer. She collapsed against his chest. "The nurses won't tell me what's going on because I'm not related to Solly and the doctor hasn't talked to me and I'm so afraid he's going to die and I'll never see him again."

"Shhhh. I'm sure Solomon will pull through. He's a fit young man." Payson wrapped his arms around Harriet and rocked her. When her trembling subsided he held her away and forced her to look at him. "Why don't I go see what I can learn about Solly's injury? You wait here in case the doctor comes out."

Harriet nodded even though she didn't see why the nurses would tell Payson any more than they'd told her. He wasn't related to Solly either.

She wondered if she should contact Solly's parents, then dismissed the idea. Her friend wouldn't appreciate waking up, only to find the man who had tried to beat him into becoming the son he wanted, in his hospital room. Solly would never forgive her.

Payson returned a short while later with news.

"The doctors have induced a coma while they work on Solly's injuries. Apparently the stream caught his side and missed his vital organs. That's the good news. He sustained extensive damage to the muscles of his left back shoulder and third degree burns to his upper left arm. He also sustained some nerve damage."

Harriet listened in horror. Her friend wouldn't be able to do his job with only one arm. She shook her head. She wouldn't think about that now. If Solly couldn't work then she would support him. He'd do the same for her if the situation was reversed.

Payson saw the head shake. "Don't worry, Harry. Solomon will get the best care available. I contacted Wade. He's flying in a burn specialist and a neurologist. The muscle tissue can be regenerated. So can the nerves. He'll have scars, and will need weeks, if not months, of physical therapy but I expect Solomon to make a full recovery."

Harriet's knees buckled. She grabbed for a nearby chair and lowered herself into it. Solly would be all right, thanks to the resort's owner, Douglas Wade.

"I owe Mr. Wade so much already." She looked up at Payson, her eyes brimming with tears. "How can I ever show Mr. Wade how much his actions mean to me? This isn't the first time he's stepped in to help when I needed it."

Payson took the seat next to Harriet. "I think Douglas knows, my dear. Don't you have a group of children arriving tomorrow? It's getting late. I think you should head back to the resort and get some sleep so you'll be ready to greet them."

Harriet shook her head. "I can't leave Solly. What if he wakes up and I'm not here? I'll tag Cassie and ask her to meet the kids."

"Those children are expecting to see you, Harry. The doctors tell me Solly will be kept in the coma for at least three days, to give his body a chance to start healing. What if I make sure Douglas's personal shuttle is available to you every evening? You can visit the hospital and personally check on Solly, maybe sit at his bedside when the doctors finish their repairs, then be back to spend the days with your kids."

Harriet took a deep breath. The children were important, but Solly was the most important person in her life. "The doctor said he's going to be in a coma for three days?"

"At least. Could be as long as five, depending on his condition."

Payson's gaze was steady. She trusted him. He wouldn't lie to her or try to manipulate her.

"Okay." She nodded. "You're right. The kids are my responsibility. It wouldn't be right to fob them off on Cassie, especially if Solly won't even know I'm here. Are you sure I'll be able to visit him every day?"

Payson smiled, creating attractive wrinkles at the outer corners of his pale blue eyes. "I promise, Harry. You can visit every day until we bring Solomon home."

"All right then." Harriet stood. "Let's go."

CHAPTER THIRTY

Three Weeks Later

"Stop babying me." Solly scowled at Harriet.

Harriet threw her hands up in the air. She'd been about to plump the couch pillows behind Solly's back. They had just eaten a dinner that she had cooked–nowhere near as good as Solly's meals, she had to admit–and she was settling him in for the night. He still had trouble sleeping and found half-sitting on the couch more restful than lying in bed where he tended to roll onto his injured shoulder.

"Well, excuse me." Harriet fisted her hands on her hips in frustration. Solly was proving to be a difficult patient. He'd only been home for three days and she already wanted to hit him with the pillows, not plump them.

Solly's expression softened. He reached out with his right hand and grabbed her hand nearest him. "I'm going to be all right, Harry," he said softly. "My physical therapist says I'm making excellent progress. I need to be doing for myself. Don't treat me like an invalid–it doesn't help."

Harriet plopped onto the floor next to the couch. "I was so afraid I was going to lose you. I hate to let you out of my sight."

Truth was, she felt exhausted. Her week with the first group of children had held a few bumps, although nothing major. The resort's employees had called the experiment a success and were ready to host another group. Harriet had divided her waking hours between the hospital and work, taking little time for sleep.

The doctors had kept Solly in a coma for six days. Six long days while she wondered if she would ever have a chance to thank her friend for saving her life.

When he finally came out of the coma they fought. Harriet scolded him for risking his life for her, and Solly lambasted Harriet for believing he would do anything less. They'd been dancing around each other and arguing ever since. Both of them were short of sleep and feeling stressed.

It was time things returned to normal, Harriet realized. She got to her feet and planted a kiss on Solly's cheek. "You're right. I need to trust that you can take care of yourself." She allowed herself a yawn. "I'll be next door if you need me. Love you."

"I'm right?" Solly grinned at her. "I'd better put this in my diary so I have a record of it."

"You don't keep a diary." Harriet heard Solly chuckle as she closed the lanai door behind her. He was going to be all right. He had some nasty scar tissue on his injured shoulder but he was quickly regaining the use of his left arm.

Once Solly was fully healed the scar tissue could be repaired if he wished. Harriet thought her friend might keep it as a badge of honor.

Harriet crossed the short distance to her own lanai and took a moment to appreciate the silvered path of the moon on the water. The breeze had died and she could hear the soft lap, lap of the waves on the beach. The night blooming jasmine vine that Solly had given her shortly after she had arrived on the island now covered one of the lanai's corner posts and perfumed the air.

A peaceful feeling stole over her, the first she'd felt in weeks.

The story of Adelaide Pelookie murdering her only child was finally beginning to die down. Ironically, Adelaide couldn't be held in one of the family prisons. She had been incarcerated in a competitor's facility instead, a facility rumored to be excessively harsh and rife with hardships.

Harriet thought it a fitting punishment.

She checked her link on her way to the bedroom and found a message from Alex.

"Harriet, it's me." A hesitation. "Payson and I need to discuss something with you. Tomorrow's fine. Give me a call in the morning. Get some sleep, sweetheart."

Harriet frowned at her link. What an odd message. Maybe they had some suggestions for the next group of underprivileged children scheduled to visit the resort next month.

She shrugged. She'd find out in the morning. Right now her king sized bed with its white, gauzy curtains beckoned.

For the the first word about releases, sales, news, and special notices, sign up for my newsletter. https://charleymarshbooks.com/mystery-newsletter/

You can find the next book in the series, *Buried in Paradise*, at your favorite retailer here: https:// books2read.com/buriedinparadise

Turn the page for a preview of the next book in the Destination Death series, *Buried in Paradise*.

BURIED IN PARADISE

"Mizz Mun-row, look at me!"

Harriet Monroe, public relations director for the Island Resort, smiled and waved enthusiastically at the young girl as she rode by on her gaily painted lion. Hayley was part of the second group of orphans Harriet had brought to the island from stateside.

Generous corporate sponsors and private donations were making her pet project of giving orphans a break from the often crowded and bleak conditions of the country's orphanages a rousing success. They had already collected enough monies to fund the project through the end of the year. Even better, the orphan's scholarship fund was keeping pace, guaranteeing a solid education for every child who desired one in the field of their choice.

Harriet took a deep breath filled with the spicy perfume of exotic flowers and let it out on a contented sigh. Ocean breezes kept the beautiful island at a comfortable eighty degrees. The Island Resort was a true paradise and she was grateful to be working there, despite some recent difficulties.

"Whee!" Happy laughter filled the air. Along with her best

friend Solomon Hayes and two other resort employees, Harriet had taken time from her other duties to escort ten of the group's twenty orphans to the resort's amusement park. She was minding three of the little girls who were riding the park's famous merry-go-round for the third time that morning.

The orphans were spending an entire week on the tropical island that was owned by the wealthiest man on the planet—her employer, the mysterious Douglas Wade. A man Harriet owed much to, but had yet to meet.

The resort hadn't been open long but was already booked solid for the next two years. Despite that, Wade had managed to make room for Harriet's orphans. She didn't know the particulars of how he had managed the feat—nor did she want to—because she'd probably feel guilty.

She imagined a few people had been told that their reservations had been cancelled due to overbooking, or some other plausible excuse. However Wade had managed it, Harriet added the orphans to the growing list of things she kept in her head that she owed her employer for.

"Mizz Mun-row!" Hayley came around again, waving madly and bouncing on her lion's back.

Harriet smiled again and waved back. She never tired of seeing the happy expressions of her orphans. This particular little girl was a real cutie with expressive brown eyes, buttery smooth caramel skin, and a gap-toothed smile that seemed undimmed by her lot in life.

One of the hotel staff had taken time from her own busy day to plait Hayley's stiff black hair into dozens of braids that stuck out all over her head like sea urchin spines tipped with bright pink ribbons. From the way Hayley kept touching her head Harriet knew no one at the orphanage had taken the time to help the little girl with her hair.

"They look like they're enjoying my merry-go-round."

Harriet turned to look up at the man standing at her side. Even though she stood nearly six foot in bare feet, Harriet had to tilt her head back to see into Braxton Holliday's smiling green eyes.

"They love it, Brax. How could they not? You did an exquisite job restoring and painting the animals. Every child we've brought here through the orphan program gravitates to the merry-go-round for a ride, and most of them ride it every day."

Braxton's fleshy lips stretched into a pleased smile. At seven foot and three hundred fifty pounds, with a gleaming shaved head and large, meaty hands, the amusement park manager looked more bear than human, but Harriet knew he had a core soft as pudding.

The merry-go-round was Braxton's pride and joy. Over three hundred years old, it had taken him years to locate and restore the animals and other parts, and it was now the only merry-go-round in operation anywhere in the world. Harriet had recently featured it in a video ad for the resort, one of her favorite ads so far.

High-pitched screams pierced the air as a short train of roller coaster cars clanked and hummed over Harriet's head. Designed by Aldous, a friend of Douglas Wade's and the world's foremost authority on historic amusement parks, the roller coaster track towered over the entire park, climbing and winding and dropping through the other rides and amusements. The coaster's high points stood so far above Harriet's head that it hurt her neck to look up at them.

With its steep climbs and stomach rolling drops it was easy to see why the coaster was a favorite with older children and adults alike.

Harriet refused to step foot on it.

Years before, when she and Solomon had been teenagers living on the streets of Portland, Maine, they had hitchhiked to a nearby beach town to eat salty potato fries and watch the amusement park rides. They had been dirt poor runaways at the time and couldn't afford to go on any of the rides–filling their bellies being much more important at the time–but Harriet never forgot the excitement and sounds of that park.

She could only imagine how exciting Braxton Holliday's park must look to the resort's visitors. The colorful park had something for everyone no matter what age. In addition to bumper cars, the park had a speedway track that circled the park's perimeter. The cars had magnetic fields that automatically fluctuated to prevent crashes, either into the low walls surrounding the track or another car.

There were gentle rides for the very young, and wild, whirly rides for older children and thrill seeking adults. Rides that whipped a person in dizzying circles and even one that dropped the brave from a hundred foot tower, only to be snapped back in a series of jerks from a thick bungee cord attached to their feet.

A soft breeze carried the scent of potato fries and grilled seafood from the food court on the edge of the park to Harriet. A resort guest could spend the entire day at the amusement park riding and eating, or they could simply relax on one of the many benches scattered through the park and watch others at play.

The merry-go-round's cheerful music wound down as it slowed to a halt. Hayley and her two companions climbed off their mounts and ran to Harriet.

"Did you see me, Miss Mun-row?" Haley asked, tugging on Harriet's hand.

Harriet placed her hand on the child's thin shoulder and gently squeezed. "I sure did. You looked magnificent riding that lion. Like the Queen of the Desert. What would you girls like to do next?"

The number of guests allowed at the resort at any one

time were limited. That prevented crowding at any of the resort's attractions. No matter what the girls decided to do, there would be no waiting in long lines.

"I want to go down the water slide." Dorian, pale and freckled with violent red hair piped up in a thin, reedy voice.

"Yeah, water slide!" Hayley and Amber Lee, the third of the trio of friends grabbed Harriet's hands and pulled.

"How about we grab a lemonade on our way there?" Harriet said hopefully. She was thirsty but took her duties as child-minder seriously and hadn't wanted to leave the girls unattended to get something to drink.

"I luuuuv lemonade," Hayley assured her.

Five minutes later Harriet and her three charges made their way over the path of crushed white shells that wound through the rides, happily sipping on ice cold, tart-sweet lemonades. She listened to the young girls chatter about the merry-go-round animals as if they were live beasts and smiled to herself. Ah, to be that young and imaginative.

The roller coaster train made a brief appearance, darting out of a thick, green grove of something Harriet couldn't identify and disappeared again. She thought she spotted Solomon's pale blue shirt in the middle car. He had volunteered to take three of the older children on the roller coaster when they begged Harriet to go with them.

She would owe him for that. And knowing her friend, he would be sure to collect. Solomon never let her get away with anything.

A frown crossed her face as she thought about her friend. She hoped he wasn't overdoing it. It had only been a few short weeks since he'd almost died from a major wound caused by a stun gun set to max.

Most of the damaged nerves and muscle tissue in Solly's back left shoulder had been replaced. Fortunately the stream from the gun had missed any vital organs. Physical therapy had worked its magic as well, but her friend still wasn't back to one hundred percent.

Solly never complained, but Harriet knew her closest friend inside and out. She could tell he still felt the effects of the injury. He also still had scar tissue, but he had decided to wait on plastic surgery, joking that the scars made him look like a badass.

And wouldn't he read her the riot act if he knew she still worried about him?

Harriet forced her thoughts back to the present. Small flowering shrubs covered in brilliant red and orange blossoms and rough-barked palm trees edged the wide path, screening it from the various rides.

Tiny, colorful birds flitted through the greenery. Brilliant green geckos darted around the palm trunks looking for prey, bobbing up and down, their bright eyes missing very little. Iridescent green and blue insects gathered pollen from large showy hibiscus blossoms.

Her little group came to a fork in the path. One fork led to the water slide, the other circled back through the park to the entrance. Wooden signs identified the paths.

"Can anyone tell me what the signs say?" Harriet asked. She dropped her empty lemonade cup into one of the park's many discreetly placed trash receptacles.

"It says . . ." Dorian scrunched her face and pointed. "That one says wa-ter-sl-ide. Water slide! That way to the water slide! Come on!" She grabbed Hayley and Amber Lee's hands and all three girls took off down the path, their thin legs flashing in the sun.

Harriet picked up the girls' dropped cups and added them to the trash bin. She knew she should scold them but decided now was not the time. She would bring up the subject of littering later and gently remind them that they needed to pick up after themselves.

She had discovered with her first group of orphans that it was difficult for them to grasp the degree of freedom they had on the island. They were used to a strictly regimented, austere life with more scolding than encouragement and few joys. As far as Harriet was concerned this week was all about bringing more joy into their difficult lives.

She set off down the water slide trail after the girls at a fast walk. Each attraction or ride at the amusement park had two employees monitoring it so Harriet wasn't worried about their safety. Other than the occasional murder, the resort had yet to lose a guest.

Most of the resort's employees had volunteered to watch over the orphans so the children wouldn't have to stay together. The extra volunteers meant a child could do whatever they wanted during their week's stay. The island had much to offer in addition to the amusement park.

The marina with every water sport toy known to man and the Angel Brothers Circus were popular destinations, as was the pristine beach that ran along the southern half of the western side of the island. Most of the orphans came from inner city neighborhoods and had never seen an ocean, let alone a beach of fine white sand. They were understandably giddy with the discovery that there was more to the world than what little they had experienced in their short lives.

Rounding a corner of lush vegetation, Harriet suddenly popped out of the jungle into a sunny clearing. The large water slide, with its labyrinth of twisting, open and covered camouflaged tubes, was part of a natural waterfall. The waterfall fed into a clear lagoon that had been altered only slightly to create shallower landing spots for the slides.

Water droplets from the waterfall's spray shimmered and sparkled in the sunlight, fracturing into miniature rainbows that formed and disappeared and formed again. Tiny lizards and birds, vibrant with color, darted through the lagoon's surrounding jungle.

The water slide was the one place in the park where the roller coaster didn't invade. The lush growth surrounding the lagoon drowned out the noise from the rest of the park and created a peaceful oasis set with well spaced benches for sitting.

Harriet waved to the water slide attendant sitting at the base of the waterfall, his feet dangling in the lagoon. The girls were already scrambling up the subtly stepped rocks to the left of the natural waterfall. Another attendant waited for them at the top to help them into the slide.

Harriet chose a bench where she could help keep an eye on the girls and made herself comfortable. The waterfall made a dull roar as it hit the lagoon, sending up a spray of fine mist. Birds sang and insects buzzed. The gentle tropical breeze rattled palm fronds over Harriet's head. The combination of mountain water and lush jungle kept the sunny spot comfortably cool.

"Mizz Mun-row! Watch me!" Hayley shouted down from the top of the waterfall. Dorian and Amber Lee waved from the openings of the two remaining slides. It looked as if the girls were going to race to the bottom.

Harriet knew that even though the three chutes criss-crossed each other several times, they were well separated at the bottom so all three girls could shoot out at the same time without fear of landing on top of each other.

"I'm watching!" Harriet shouted back. She gave a double thumbs up sign and settle back to wait for the girls to reappear at the bottom.

Amber Lee and Dorian popped up in the lagoon several minutes later but there was no sign of Hayley. Harriet jumped to her feet. The lagoon attendant was on his feet, wading towards the spot where Hayley should have appeared.

"Do you see her?" Harriet called. Fear clutched at her heart. She knew the water in the slide was shallow, making drowning difficult. But what if Hayley had bumped her head somehow?

"No." The attenant shook his head. "She should have popped out by now, unless she deliberately stopped herself. The kids do that sometimes. The slide is clear until it reaches the last ten feet, so you feel like you're inside the waterfall. It's pretty cool. You should try it." The attendant didn't sound worried at all.

Harriet relaxed slightly. There wasn't anything in the slide to hurt Hayley. The attendant most likely had the right of it, Hayley had spread her hands and feet to stop her slide down the tube.

"I wonder how long she can hold herself up there?"

The attendant shrugged. "She's young so probably not more than a few minutes. There's a sharp curve on a fairly level section of the tube that's a little slower. My guess is that's where she is. I'll go–" he stopped talking abruptly.

"What is it?" And then Harriet saw for herself. An adult-sized body had popped out of the end of the slide, followed immediately by a scowling Hayley.

"That man blocked my slide," she complained as she waded toward the edge of the lagoon. "I had to push him to make him get going. I want to go again."

Harriet barely heard her. She was staring in horror at the body floating face down in the lagoon.

A body with a massive dent in the back of his head.

Timberdoodle Press

P.O. Box 194

Houston, MN 55943

timberdoodle@goacentek.net

Print Book ISBN# 978-1-945856-72-3

Cover Art: nordenworks.gmail.com /depositphotos.com

ABOUT THE AUTHOR

In her younger days Charley Marsh's curiosity drove her to climb mountains, canoe rivers, and explore caves and wilderness areas from Maine to California. She's been shot at, caught in a desert flash flood, and almost drowned off the Maine coast. Once she tobogganed down a 5,000+ foot mountain.

Life is always an adventure if you have the right attitude.

Charley never set out to be a storyteller, but looking back on the elaborate lies she made up as a troubled teen she can see that she always had the makings. Now, in the words of Lawrence Block, she happily "makes up lies for fun and profit."